The Girl in Black

The Girl in Black

Angela Bianchini

a translation of
La ragazza in nero
by

Giuliana Sanguinetti Katz
and
Anne Urbancic

CANADIAN SOCIETY FOR ITALIAN STUDIES

The Italian edition of Angela Bianchini's *La ragazza in nero*
©2002 Edizioni Frassinelli S.r.l.

The English translation of Angela's Bianchini, *La ragazza in nero (The Girl in Black)* ©2002 by Giuliana Sanguinetti Katz and Anne Urbancic.

Book Layout and Cover Illustration/Design:
Michelle V. Lohnes

CANADIAN SOCIETY FOR ITALIAN STUDIES

P.O. Box 847
Welland, Ontario
Canada L3B 5Y5

ISBN 0-921831-91-9   Printed in Canada

National Library of Canada Cataloguing in Publication

Bianchini, Angela
    The girl in black / Angela Bianchini; translated by
Giuliana Sanguinetti Katz and Anne Urbancic.

Translation of: La ragazza in nero.

ISBN 0-921831-91-9

    I. Sanguinetti Katz, Giuliana II. Urbancic, Anne,
1954- III. Canadian Society for Italian Studies IV. Title.

PQ4862.I2R3413 2002   853'.914   C2002-905346-3

CONTENTS

ANGELA BIANCHINI'S LIFE AND WORKS

Angela Bianchini was born in Rome in a Jewish family, grew up there and emigrated to the United States in 1941, after Mussolini's racial laws were enacted. These laws were openly anti-Semitic. She spent her "years of waiting" (to use Giovanni Macchia's· expression) at Johns Hopkins University where she completed a Ph.D. in French Linguistics under the guidance and supervision of Leo Spitzer. The presence and lectures of an exceptional group of Spanish exiles (among whom Pedro Salinas and Jorge Guillén) determined some of her major interests in the field of Spanish literature: in particular the great XXth century poetry and XIXth century novel.

After her return to Rome after the war, Angela Bianchini was attracted to the world of communication and collaborated not only with such prestigious periodicals as *Il mondo di Pannunzio*, but also with RAI (the Italian Broadcasting Corporation). For RAI she wrote several cultural broadcasts, radio plays and original radio and T.V. programs.

She also has many literary studies to her credit. She was one of the first critics to study serial novels in *La luce a gas e il feuilleton: due invenzioni dell'Ottocento* (Liguori, 1969, reprinted in 1989). She translated Medieval French novels (*Romanzi medievali d'amore e d'avventura*, Grandi Libri Garzanti, now reprinted and in CD-ROM), and edited a Renaissance correspondence (*Lettere della fiorentina Alessandra Macinghi Strozzi*, Garzanti 1989). In her recent book *Voce donna* (Frassinelli 1979, reprinted in 1996) she combines a study of feminism with her interests in biography and in narrative technique. For the past thirty years she has contributed to *La Stampa* (Turin) and to its book-review section *Tuttolibri*, especially on Spanish themes.

Angela Bianchini began her career in fiction with the short stories of *Lungo equinozio* (Lerici 1962; Senator Borletti Prize for a First Work, 1962), which deal with the lives of women who live in Italy and in America. Here for the first time she explores her recurring theme of departures and arrivals. Giorgio Caproni, in a book review, comments enthusiastically on Bianchini's technique and on the texture of her stories, composed of everyday sentences and of scattered events against which stand out significant figures and particular historical moments (*La Nazione*, 10 May 1962). Carlo Bo, on the other hand, praises Bianchini's knowledge of the human heart and her sincerity and literary authenticity (*L'Europeo*, 7 October 1962). Recently Bianchini has contributed the short story "Alta estate notturna" to the anthology of women writers *Il pozzo segreto*, ed. M. R.Cutrufelli, R. Guacci, M. Rusconi, Giunti 1993 and the short story "Anni dopo" ("Years Later") to the anthology *Nella città proibita*, ed. M.R. Cutrufelli, Tropea 1997 (*In the Forbidden City*, University of Chicago Press 2000).

Bianchini has also written several novels. In *Le nostre distanze* (Mondadori 1965, reprinted by Einaudi in 2001) she narrates the experiences of a young woman, an Italian student at a university in the United States, during the Second World War. Paolo Milano writes about the novel: "In the shadow of a prestigious professor, and in the net of an ambiguous friendship, she lives and suffers through all the problems of a difficult growth: bitter eradication, religious anxieties (she seeks a refuge in catholicism), and especially emotional loss" (Paolo Milano, *L'Espresso*, 27 March 1965). And in a recent entry for the *Dizionario delle opere della letteratura italiana*, edited by Alberto Asor Rosa (Einaudi 2000) Chiara Agostinelli describes the "contrast between the almost fairytale world of the university campus and the squalor of the surrounding areas" as well as the "crisis of a generation unsettled and uprooted by the violence of war".

In *La ragazza in nero* (*The Girl in Black*, Camunia 1990, Rapallo Prize 1990), which is the story of a girl in search of maternity, the author combines reality, symbols and images in the life of a modern girl, against the background of Rome. As Giulio Cattaneo points out, the main event of the novel is the protagonist's decision to have a child, determined by her partly real, partly imaginary encounter with the mysterious girl in black (Introduction to *Capo d'Europa e altre storie*, Bompiani 1992).

Her subsequent novel, *Capo d'Europa*, (Camunia 1991, reprinted by Frassinelli Tascabile 1998, finalist for the Strega Prize 1991, Donna-Città di Roma Prize 1992, translated as *The Edge of Europe* by A. M. Jeannet and D. Castronuovo, University of Nebraska Press 2000), takes place in Lisbon, a stopping place for a Jewish girl running away from Europe to America during World War II. Furio Colombo reminds us that this is the only testimonial in Italian literature of the emigration caused by Italian racial laws and defines the novel "a little jewel" (Furio Colombo, *La Stampa*, 25 January 1993). And Laura Mancinelli speaks of "the sorrow that is hidden under the polished pages of the novel" and sees in the protagonist "a tragic manifestation of the way violence can silence even the most human feelings" (Laura Mancinelli, *L'Indice dei Libri del Mese*, June 1991).

Le labbra tue sincere (Frassinelli 1995) takes place in Rome, during the *Belle Epoque*, when Giolitti was prime minister in Italy. It describes the amorous encounter between a sensual and restless lady from Turin and an American writer. He has come back to Rome, drawn by memory and nostalgia, whereas she has apparently come to the capital in order to follow the artistic education of her two adolescent daughters. According to Giorgio Barberi Squarotti "it is a novel about shadowy feelings, life secrets kept hidden by the discretion of social conventions and suddenly revealed by a chance encounter, a conversation or increased heart beat due to illusions or disappointments...." (Giorgio Barberi Squarotti, *La Stampa*, 25 February 1995).

And finally, *Un amore sconveniente* (Frassinelli 1999, Castiglioncello Costa degli Etruschi Prize 2000, finalist for the Rapallo Prize 2000) retraces much of the twentieth century's dramatic history, while following the *amour fou* between a Jewish man who is an antifascist and liberal intellectual and a fatal and mysterious woman. Giorgio Calcagno observes that the charm of the novel consists in the doubling up of the story into the events which are described and those that are alluded to by the author: "These continuous refractions from one story to the other multiply the possible interpretations" (Giorgio Calcagno, *Tuttolibri*, 30 October 1999). Maria Rosa Cutrufelli remarks that here, in contrast with her previous works, the author takes over the male point of view and explores it in depth (Maria Rosa Cutrufelli, *Il diario della settimana*, 12 January 2000).

Text by Angela Bianchini, translated by G. Sanguinetti Katz and A. Urbancic.

Bibliography of *La ragazza in nero*

Barberi Squarotti, Giorgio. "Bianchini: fine di una solitudine." *La Stampa*, 3 marzo 1990.

Campana, Stefanella. "Vita cambiata da una ragazza in nero." *Stampa Sera*, 12 febbraio 1990.

Cutrufelli, Maria Rosa. "Quel sottile bisogno di vita quotidiana." *L'Unità*, 1 aprile 1990.

Debenedetti Antonio. "Angela, Alice: da Roma a New York." *Corriere della Sera*, 10 giugno 1990.

Jeannet, Angela M. "Afterword: Exiles and Returns in Angela Bianchini's Fiction." in Angela Bianchini, *The Edge of Europe*. Trans. by A. M. Jeannet and D. Castronuovo. Lincoln and London: University of Nebraska Press, 2000, pp. 105-37.

Massari, Giulia. "Nonna, madre, figlia." *Il Giornale*, 25 marzo 1990.

Pederiali, Giuseppe. "Il mondo tutto al femminile." *Il Giorno*, 18 febbraio 1990.

Reverdito, Guido. "Narrativa italiana." *Leggere*, giugno 1990.

Trotta, Donatella. "Fate bimbi, non libri. L'utopia solitaria della ragazza in nero." *Il Mattino*, 13 marzo 1990.

THE SEARCH FOR IDENTITY
IN ANGELA BIANCHINI'S
The Girl in Black

Usually the female protagonists of Bianchini's novels are women oppressed by a rigid upbringing and traumatized by private and historical events. Compelled to give up their private life and loves by rigid societal conventions (*Le labbra tue sincere*), or torn away from their family and city by racial laws and the horrors of WWII (*Gli Oleandri*, *Capo d'Europa* [*The Edge of Europe*]), these women try in vain to integrate their past rich in memories and affections with their lonely and painful present.[1] Their effort to find a personal identity and make contact with reality fails: they either remain frozen in a state of shock when confronted with despair and death (*The Edge of Europe*), or they take refuge in dreams and memories that go back to childhood games (*Gli oleandri*).

In *Gli oleandri* Walter, the protagonist's lover, comforts her after the death of her best friend Orietta by telling her that only fairytales, stories and films matter in this life: "Love, life itself, is always like your childhood dresses: you cut them, sew them, model them, decorate them, adjust them until they fit you perfectly, until you think that they fit you perfectly, until they really are all yours" (Bianchini, 90; the translation is mine).

In contrast with these girls who are lost forever in past dreams or fixated on some painful moments of their life, the protagonist of *The Girl in Black* manages to detach herself from her family and integrate her present and her past as a necessary prelude to finding her identity. Though nameless like the protagonists of *The Edge of Europe* and of *Gli oleandri* and often as lonely and anxious as they are, she gains a sense of independence and an awareness of her femininity that the other women lack. It is her decision to have a child and her experience with her baby that bring about a new sense of self and allow her to come to terms with the painful memories of her youth and with her difficult relationship with her mother.

The main subject of the novel is the changing relationship among three women of the same family: the protagonist, simply called "the girl," and her mother and grandmother who are seen through the eyes of the girl. The novel develops like an inner monologue, where the girl relives the difficult moments of her childhood and adolescence through a long and difficult winter, alone with her baby, as a single mother in a gloomy apartment in Rome.

The protagonist was born in postwar Italy to an Italian middle class woman and an American officer who returned to America, remarried and never saw his daughter again. She spends her early childhood in a family made up entirely of women and feels different from the other children she meets. She is painfully aware that she has no father and that she does not fit either with the Italian or with the American children because she is half American and half Italian. She is especially aware of being an outcast in the American school she attends in her early childhood.

Her mother is a rigid, anxious, obsessive person, who acts out of duty and torments all the members of her family, including her weak second husband Giovanni. Her maternal grandmother, on the other hand, is a very beautiful, charming and elegant woman, who seems to be ageless. She has a lover, Enzo, who is younger than her own daughter. In fact, for the girl, she is like an ideal mother, one who never blames her for anything, understands all her needs and gives her what she wants. She even seems to encourage the girl's infatuation for Enzo by discussing her own sexual attachment to him when the girl is around. Her lover Enzo, as handsome and generous as grandmother, appears to the girl as the ideal father she would like to have, who has come to fill the void left by her real father and who is quite different from her boring and insipid stepfather, Giovanni. From the age of eleven she has sexual fantasies about Enzo every night and hopes to be taken by him into a world of pleasure, in the same way as her grandmother. Yet even the charming Enzo, after a few years of an intense relationship with grand-mother, leaves her suddenly and disappears, causing her to age overnight and lose all her pleasure in life.

Relationships among women are at the centre of the story, especially the tight bond between mother and daughter: the girl with her mother and the mother, in turn, with her own mother. The closeness between these three women is brought about in part by the displaced and precarious life that the mother had to lead, first when she travelled from Italy to America, and later when she was deserted by her American husband. This exclusive bond is full of a mixture of love and resentment as the mother tries to control both the girl and the grandmother and to organize their life, while disapproving of any man that may come into the picture and threaten to occupy their thoughts. In her turn, the girl would like to be free and independent, but she also resents her mother's new hus-band, who separates her from her mother without providing her with a new parental figure.

Only at the end of the novel, when the protagonist relives her own childhood years through her daughter Prisca, does she allow herself to remember a very different image of her mother as an attractive, carefree and desir-able woman. This image appears in the dreamlike memory of the days when, as a little child, she and her mother attended the traditional spring fair held at the American school, "a rural celebration of spring and summer" that "belonged only to the two of them" (Bianchini, 203). In those magic days, mother and daughter were united by their special awareness of the significance of the fair as a traditional festival: all their difficulties overcome, they finally felt accepted by the American community and shared the impossible dream of a future with a transitory group of people, who were bound to return soon to Amer-ica, once their stay in Italy was over.

It is this original blissful union that is at the basis of any subsequent close relationship, in particular that of the girl with her grandmother, who is for her more like a fairy godmother than a real human being. And it is the loss of that closeness with mother (represented symbolically by the girl's loss of appetite for a favourite food when she hears the news of her mother's imminent marriage) which is the model for subsequent losses: grandmother's many departures in spring, her sudden death after Prisca's birth, and the disappearance of the girl's boyfriends, Sergio and Luigi.

The key scene in the story takes place towards the beginning of the novel, when the twenty four year old protagonist, temporarily free from her duties as a school-teacher, finds herself wandering on a foggy November morning through Villa Borghese, towards the Italian garden in front of the Museum. The memories of past happiness flood her mind: her romantic walks with her boyfriend Sergio when she was an adolescent, and her childhood games in that garden when the family maid Cesira took her there. In those memories the garden appears as a lost paradise full of "violets, gillyflowers, carnations, and unknown flowers in carpets decorated with arabesques" surrounding a central basin where the children's toy boats "rocked, balancing softly on the water, wedged against the water lilies" (Bianchini 113).

But just as the girl's past happiness is contrasted with her present loneliness, boredom and disgust with her life, so the beautiful memories of the garden are contrasted with its present state of abandonment and disrepair: the flowers have been replaced by bits of shrivelled grass, the water of the basin is "dirty greenish" with "dirty bits of paper floating on top and even more of them lying on the bottom," and the wooden benches are splintered (Bianchini, 113). Yet some traces of its past splendour remain. In the same way the protagonist feels that something wonderful will happen to her.

While she sits surrounded by strange visions that appear to her behind the Museum's windows and seem like fragments of her own past, she feels her period coming on as a "sweet languor" which runs through her body "like an inner river which melted inside her and fertilized her." It gives her a sense of awakening and of fulfilment (Bianchini, 114). But she quickly realizes that her hope to recreate her happy past by watching children play in the garden is destined to be disappointed: the garden is completely empty and the girl is all alone "in the damp and inhospitable cold" which penetrates her (Bianchini, 115).

At this precise moment, when she is about to leave the garden, from that part of the garden she has not yet explored, where the road is "flanked by a white banister of griffins and lions, dominated by two curious structures... identified only as places of delight, enchantment and mystery" there appears a "dark spectre" in the white fog. This strange creature which advances slowly appears to be a composite figure and has a smaller shape and face in front, but stretches out "immensely behind its head, like a camel, so as to render everything absolutely unknown, unreal" (Bianchini, 115-16). As the fog lifts, the strange centaur-like figure becomes first a black bandit with a Calabrian hat, wheeling a child on a bicycle, then a woman with a man's hat and a tight black velvet jacket in the style of the forties, and finally an attractive girl with "a mass of raven hair" hidden under her hat, framing "her dark, oval, Mediterranean face" (Bianchini, 116-18). The girl in black is clearly an excellent mother to her little child: she feeds him, plays with him and is obviously delighted by everything he does. At the same time, with her masculine appearance, her frank, even aggressive manners, and her open contempt of men in general and the child's father in particular, she indicates to the protagonist that motherhood can be a woman's decision and that a woman can take over the role of mother and father to the newborn child.

What we have in this extended dreamlike sequence is a condensation of the protagonist's fears and hopes and an attempt at finding a resolution. The strange figure with its mixture of pleasant connotations (it appears against the background of two pavilions which are "places of delight") and frightening ones (it is a strange "dark spectre" that keeps changing in shape) seems to indicate a

primal scene, seen through the eyes of a child, where
father and mother making love become a strange, composite creature.[2] The frightening elements refer to the
earlier fantasies of the protagonist concerning mother's
sexual life, her unavailable father, and her mother's boyfriends. The pleasant pavilions refer to grandmother's
view of love and sexuality as a "fountain of youth" and a
source of earthly delights (Bianchini, 137). The composite
figure alludes to the pregnant mother (two figures in one)
and to the mother giving birth to a child, with the head of
the child protruding from the mother's body (the small
head sticking out of the strange elongated body). Once
more, pleasant and frightening associations accompany
this fantasy of childbirth.

Finally the figure of the girl in black, who is in turn a
bandit with a child, a woman with a man's hat and finally
an attractive young woman with long black hair, alludes
to the fantasy of parthenogenesis on the part the protagonist: a fantasy of being self sufficient, of giving birth to
another self and recreate the original mother-child unit,
without the danger of being disappointed and abandoned. It is a fantasy of being both mother and father to
the child, beautiful, strong and terrifying to others, rather
than weak and dependent on parental figures.[3]

This fantasy leads the protagonist to embark on a relationship with a young man devoted to social causes but
unable to face his own family life, and therefore not ready
for the role of father figure. In fact in her choice of a companion she duplicates the experience not only of the girl
in black but also of her own mother, prematurely divorced
from her American husband. With great rapidity she carries her plan into action, becomes pregnant and has a
child who is born prematurely, at seven months. In spite
of her joy at having a baby, she is compelled to face the
loneliness of being a single parent who lives on her own,
since she does not want to live with her mother and rees-
tablish her painful closeness to her. Her loneliness is
accentuated by the loss of grandmother, who dies shortly
after Prisca's birth. The death of this ideal parental figure,
which occurs unexpectedly after the baby's birth, might
represent the end of the girl's adolescent fantasies when

these are confronted by the reality of a baby in need of her constant care.

During the painful months of the first winter spent with Prisca in the isolation of her little apartment, the girl reflects over her past life, and tries to come to terms with it and understand herself. Gradually the pleasure of seeing her daughter grow and develop into a bright and beautiful child, in spite of her premature birth, gives her the sense of joy and self-worth she lacked before. This experience, moreover, brings her close to her own mother, who loves Prisca and relives with her the happiness and pride she felt when she took care of her own child. At the end of this long and difficult winter, the protagonist has two encounters that signal to her an inner change. While she is driving in the centre of Rome, she catches sight of a woman at a bus stop who reminds her of the girl in black. The girl has a masculine look and is wearing a tight-wasted raincoat, trousers, a heavy sweater and the wide-brimmed man's hat she was wearing the first time. This time, however, "on the nape of her neck. ... there escaped some rebellious curly hair" which "in its curious vitality sent a message: beauty and love" (Bianchini, 197).

The second encounter takes place shortly after, when at the end of winter the protagonist visits a clothes store displaying all the new spring fashion. She finds herself surrounded by a fantastic world of mannequins, portraying adolescent girls performing all possible activities and wearing imaginative and bright coloured garments. Here the protagonist, who feels too old and out of place to wear such playful clothes, meets a young salesgirl, who persuades her to try some light, springlike clothes. When the protagonist complains that they are transparent, the salesgirl replies that all she needs is matching underwear. "With a sharp movement she pulled down the zipper of her jeans and revealed a very white little belly and black pubic hair escaping out of her yellow g-string"(Bianchini, 218).

These two encounters reflect the protagonist's changed state of mind: the girl in black shows a touching element of femininity in the hair on the nape of her neck under her masculine hat, and the young salesgirl stresses the protagonist's right to be young and carefree by encouraging her to buy attractive clothes and showing her her pubic hair. The protagonist at this point moves from the previous ideal of a masculine and dominating self (embodied by the girl in black) to a more feminine view of her capacities, even if she is still fascinated by the idea of a strong female model. The salesgirl, in fact, combines the charm and carefree attitude of adolescence with an aggressive behaviour that is symbolically portrayed by her Medusa hairstyle, which links her to the Medusa like appearance of the girl in black.[4] The girl's desire to renew herself, her hope for an imminent spring and especially her new trust in her mother, who now seems to her more like her beloved grandmother, are all signs of a happier stage in life on the way to a newly found maturity and identity. In the last scene of the novel the girl walks home in the snow excited by her new spring clothes. She thinks of the dress that she will buy for Prisca: mother and daughter are seen here united in the protagonist's mind in the anticipation of a happy future together.

Giuliana Sanguinetti Katz

Works Cited

Bianchini, Angela. *Capo d'Europa e altre storie*. Milano: Bompiani, 1992. It has an introduction by Giulio Cattaneo and includes *Gli oleandri, La ragazza in nero* and *Capo d'Europa*, which were published separately by Camunia editrice, respectively in 1962, 1990 and 1991.

Chasseguet-Smirgel, Janine. "Freud and Female Sexuality" in *Sexuality and Mind*. New York: New York University Press,1986, pp. 9-28.

—-."The Archaic Matrix of the Oedipus Complex" in *Sexuality and Mind*, pp. 74-91.

Deutsch, Helene. *Psychology of women*. 2 vols. New York: Grune & Stratton, 1944-45.

Du Bois, Page. *Sowing the Body. Psychoanalysis and Ancient Representations of Women*. Chicago: The University of Chicago Press, 1988.

Elias-Button, Karen. "The Muse as Medusa," in *The Lost Tradition*. Eds. Cathy N. Davidson and E. M. Broner. New York: Frederick Ungar Publishing Co., 1980, pp. 193-206,

Jeannet,Angela M., "Afterword: Exiles and Returns in Angela Bianchini's Fiction." in Angela Bianchini. *The Edge of Europe*. Trans.

A.M. Jeannet and D. Castronuovo. Licoln and London: University of Nebraska Press, 2000.

Reik, Theodor. *Dogma and Compulsion*. Westport: Greenwood Press, 1973.

Notes

1.   For a treatment of the theme of exile in Bianchini's work see Angela Jeannet, "Afterword: Exiles and Returns in Angela Bianchini's Fiction."

2.   The monster made of different parts can be compared with the Sphinx which Reik in his article "Oedipus and the Sphinx" sees as a condensation of the fantasies of the child "who observes the sexual intercourse of adults" interprets it as an act of aggression and "identifies himself not only with the father, but also with the mother" (327).

3.   Helene Deutsch in *Psychology of Women*, vol. 2, p. 16, observes that "in modern women often we find the fantasy of the parthenogenetic child, born of the masculine wish in woman for power of her own and complete independence of man, or an even deeper and more complex psychological process."
Chasseguet-Smirgel in "Freud and Female Sexuality" (27-28) and "The Archaic Matrix of the Oedipus Complex" (77) explains that penis-envy in the woman may be due to the desire of triumphing over a domineering mother, by having the organ the mother lacks, as well as to the fear of father's sexuality (fear of rape and murder).

4.   Page du Bois interprets the image of Medusa in ancient Greece as "the image of the mother who is parthenogenetic, like the earth, or who is androgynous, equipped with a snake/phallus" (91).
Karen Elias-Button in "The Muse as Medusa" discusses two sides of Medusa, seen as the "grasping mother, representative of the entanglements mothers and daughters encounter so often" and also as "a metaphor for powers previously hidden and denigrated, collective powers we are finally beginning to reaffirm and claim for ourselves" (194).

MEMORY IN
The Girl in Black

As I reflect on the role of memory in Angela Bianchini's *The Girl in Black*, I am reminded of the apocryphal story about the young man who wanted his new bride to cook the roast exactly as he remembered his mother had prepared it. Although she followed the same recipe, the young wife could never get it quite right until finally, in tears, she asked her mother-in-law for advice. It was then that the young woman discovered from the mother-in-law that the latter was a terrible cook who used to burn the dinner on a regular basis. But the young man never recalled any burnt dinners and insisted that mother had prepared only delicious meals.

The tasty roast was only the memory thereof, a story about the young man's childhood. All our memories are the stories that we tell ourselves. They involve secrets that are no longer, time that perhaps never was, knowledge that is not fact. But paradoxically neither is it fiction. As with all stories, memories are amorphous and take on differing shapes each time we recall them: sometimes sadder, sometimes happier, sometimes longer, sometimes more succinct. We tell ourselves these stories in order to better understand ourselves, or to justify ourselves to our own hearts and minds. As with all stories, memory needs a language, as Patricia Hampl writes in her study on memory, *I Could Tell You Stories*,

> we wish to talk to each other about life and death, about love, despair, loss, and innocence. We sense that in order to live together we must learn to speak of peace, of history, of meaning and values. The big words. We seek a means of exchange, a language which will renew these ancient concerns and make them wholly, pulsingly ours. Instinctively, we go to our store of private associations for our authority to speak of these weighty issues. We find, in our details and broken, obscured

images, the language of symbol. Here memory impulsively
reaches out and embraces imagination. That is the resort to invention. It isn't a lie, but an act of necessity, as the innate urge
to locate truth always is (31).

Like memories, people too change with time. The person I
was twenty years ago certainly is not the person I am today; nor am I now the person I will be twenty years from
today. Isn't curious that in reliving the memories of who I
was and what I did long ago, I can see the traces of the person I am at the present time and I can project forward to
envisage who I will be in the future? Or, rather more or less
the person I was and shall become. And there lies the most
important factor of memory: it is always more or less, it is
never precise. Feedback, or remembering the past, and its
complement, feedforward, or imagining the future, are
never in documentable fact but always in blurred sensory
perception. They are always vague, and unprovable.

Memories are also the stories that the girl, the protagonist of Bianchini's novel, tells herself in order to
understand herself better, to understand her place in her
world, just as Hampl indicates in the quote above. Memories help the girl understand those fundamental
concepts of life that Hampl refers to as "the big words".
The importance of memory in its imprecise and often
onyric dimensions is underscored from the very beginning of this work in Bianchini's refusal to name her
protagonist, thereby never giving her the specificity of a
precise identity. Likewise in the author's refusal to give the
girl a "proper" father. Instead, her father becomes known
to her only through his absence, or mediated by the memories of the mother. The girl has never experienced what
the French psychoanalyst and philosopher Jacques Lacan
referred to as "the name of the father", that unwritten Law
that in our unconscious firmly establishes for us all our
identity in our social environment. It comes as no surprise, therefore, that the girl has no such environment,
but passes, almost as in a dream from one situation to
another: from America (that land of dreams for postwar
Italians), to the magical gardens of the Villa Borghese, to
the enchantment of the summer fair at the American
school (which in the manner of an Italian version of Briga-

doon appears for only one day a year and then disappears), to the evasive and fairy-like figure of Grandmother. That reality and memory are firmly separated and irrevocably divorced in her understanding is evident even in the fact that in her 'real' life, that life of responsibility as a single parent with a young child, the girl distances herself from all her places of memory and goes to live, on her own with her child, in an isolated apartment that, as Bianchini writes, left her with the impression of having emigrated to another continent. But without her places of memory, the girl lived only half a life; she did not have a full grasp of herself and her situation, just as from her new, distant apartment she could not appreciate a full view of her environment since her windows allowed her to see only the tops of the heads of passersby and only the roofs of cars streaming past.

Bianchini's novel is developed on several intersecting planes of memory. Primarily the memories are gynocentric, involving the various female characters as girls, lovers, or mothers/grandmothers[1]. This is not unusual given that Mnemosyne, the Titaness who bestowed the gift of memory upon humankind and who is also the mother of the Muses, is clearly a female figure. The one woman who is the exception and who does not participate in recounting her memories is the mysterious girl in black. She is a dark Madonna with her baby who is the only female figure without memories, perhaps because she belongs only to the girl's memory and not to her reality. She belongs, that is to say, to that one single moment of the meeting in the park between her and the girl on a misty November morning. She is like the perfect Venus, whose statue in the park, with its marble curls escaping down the nape of her neck, presages her arrival (Bianchini 110). The girl in black stands out so strikingly precisely because of her refusal of memory. Nonetheless, while she herself has no memories to share, she becomes the principal element in the memory of the protagonist. The first appearance of the girl in black shows how she is, in fact, part of an undefined collective memory: she slowly advances out of the late autumnal fog as if she were some kind of proteiform creature (an element outside of recorded memory), then a centaur (belonging to mythical memory), to finally become a mother and baby (in this role the girl in black awakens in the protagonist the memory of desire that had always been deeply repressed). The casual reference the girl in black makes to her baby's father in dismissing him as just some guy clearly shows that she carries no emotional baggage of mental souvenirs with her. This is why she is such an effective catalyst for the girl who has no choice but to accept her as she is, there in the garden of the Villa Borghese, unbound by any ties that may link her to other times, or to other people and places, ties that could be examined, and analyzed for ulterior motives and intentions. For the protagonist, there is no possibility of belaboring the reasons behind the fatalistic and sudden declaration of the girl in black that she, the protagonist, needed a baby of her own. Furthermore, the declaration was made just in the moments that the girl felt her period coming on, moments which reinforced in her the existence of a deep inner world of her self-acceptance of womanhood. The fatalistic declaration, made outside of any previous context, could not speak to the girl's rational, objective world of facts or documents, but only to her memories and desires.

The story of the girl is not recounted in a diachronic or linear narrative, but rather through a series of remembered vignettes. As with our own memories, the chronology of these is somewhat displaced. For this reason we have, therefore, her announcement of her pregnancy to Grandmother, followed much later and in much greater detail, by her memories of her affair with Luigi. Together, the jumbles of remembered vignettes represent the fundamental moments of the girl's coming to womanhood. Each memory is independent of the others, but as the girl recalls them, we fill in the missing links to complete and smooth out her story. These are not simply casual reminiscences, but rather, they act as a life review for the protagonist. Cognitive psychologists differentiate between the two by ascribing to reminiscence a high level of spontaneity, whose triggers are many and varied. A life review, on the other hand, is much less spontaneous; its triggers are more specific and generally represent perceived milestones that point to a life crisis or a transition, and that usually require a self reassessment. Echoing the words of Patricia Hampl, psychologists Jeffrey D. Webster and Barbara Haight observe that in a life review

> [t]here is also a greater effort to evaluate the recalled memories in order to derive a sense of meaning and purpose to one's life. This necessarily entails working through painful emotional episodes as well as positive, self-enhancing memories. Evaluation involves renegotiating the meaning of memories given their psychosociocultural origins" (77).

In Bianchini's novel, the protagonist herself has taught us how to proceed as we read in filling in the missing elements between one reminiscence and the next in order to re-evaluate the history of her womanhood. For example, she recalls for us how she met the girl in black who told her she ought to experience maternity. She also recalls that at that particular time her period was beginning. And in her memory she establishes the link between the two events, assigning them a milestone importance that leads her to make the decision that changes her life:

> When she started towards the gate, the world was profoundly changed. She raised her eyes to look at the sky: it was a deep blue, as if summer or spring had come back. Or an unknown season with a gentle warmth. I have to go home, she thought: I can do what I want I can decide for myself. I'm going to put myself at the centre of the world and arrange everything around me. (p.124).

Likewise, we as the readers privy to her memories, also make the links between them. Such is the manner, for instance, in which we almost unconsciously complete the story of Grandmother and Enzo. It is through the juxtaposition of two separate recollections that we discover that Grandmother and Enzo have ended their love affair. In the summer during which the girl had fallen in love with Sergio, she hoped to convince Grandmother to entreat Mother for permission to travel with Sergio to Sardinia. But then two fundamental events occur: the first is her chance meeting with Enzo at which he tells her that he doesn't know when he and Grandmother would be departing for their annual holiday. This chance meeting is truly a signal of how memories act as a life review, because at first, the girl does not acknowledge its importance to her, telling us only that "one year Grandmother did not leave. During that year Enzo no longer came to visit her. He never came again" (Bianchini, 107). Only later does she reveal that she did in fact see Enzo during this time.

The second fundamental event that allows us to know the story of the two lovers, is Grandmother's initial refusal to help the protagonist convince her mother to let her join Sergio in Sardinia. The protagonist remembers that Grandmother had said 'no'

> without even saying darling, darling, don't cry, don't get upset. The girl had remained there, with the black phone receiver in her hand, not understanding (Bianchini, 135).

In linking these two memories we as readers confirm the end of Grandmother's love affair with Enzo. A similar linking of two memories occurs also later on in the novel when the protagonist thinks that she sees the girl in black once more. The girl in black is waiting for a bus; she is dressed differently now and has no baby in her arms. In the hesitant and seductive moments of early spring, the memory of the girl in black who had exhorted her to have a baby changes, and in the curls of black hair that escape from under the hat of the girl at the bus stop, the protagonist feels not the need for defining her womanhood through maternity but through beauty and love. She suddenly recalls Grandmother's perfume, a scent of violets, and she becomes aware also that the memory of the perfume brings with it the memory of desire. The chapter ends with our linking the two memories, and making of them a story of hope: "even more secret patterns might appear, and other desires for love, buried under the leafage of so many seasons, might come back to life."(Bianchini, p. 199). It is interesting to note that at this meeting too, the girl in black refuses again to belong to memory: the protagonist is never sure whether it is indeed she, the girl of the park at Villa Borghese, or whether it is someone else completely different.

As is the protagonist, so are the other women of the novel dependent on telling their stories through memory and implied reminiscences. Even the minor female characters are allowed moments of memories, as is the case for

Grandmother's nurse, Anna, for whom Grandmother's armchair is a source of reminiscence (Bianchini, 140), and for Grandmother's cousin, Nenè, surrounded by her travel brochures and photographs, all souvenirs recalling her various trips (Bianchini, 168). Often, the reminiscences are filtered still further through the memories of the protagonist as well, rendering them more unclear and more chaotic. Cesira the domestic, for example, is a remembered figure from the girl's childhood but who is allowed her own memories. The relevance of Cesira's reminiscences is often obscure to the novel's protagonist. Thus when the domestic laughingly claims that the fountain of youth works wonders on women's skin, the girl, who is not privy to Cesira's memories, remembers instead how Grandmother had playfully alluded to Enzo as a fountain of youth. Through these seemingly unconnected recollections, we as readers fill in the gaps of the relationship between Enzo and Grandmother.

Mother relives her whole life through memory. Although she has remarried and has established herself again as the wife of the dentist Giovanni, it is the memories of the girl's father, the American, that continue to motivate her. Some of these are "invented" memories of a male figure, used as a self defense mechanism in order to satisfy the gossipy neighbours: she "felt badly ... and offered various anxious explanations [saying] the child's father visited often and was very affectionate...." (Bianchini, p.97) The memories of the girl's father bring into play for Mother her own memories of an absent father, a man who apparently had died when she was still very young. For Mother, the memories are of a loving man; Grandmother, however, refuses "that faded image" of a husband who died prematurely, although she does allow Mother her memories, even if they might be "invented" ones (Bianchini, p.128).

Grandmother too, is a woman of memories, memories of which she is the perennial youthful protagonist. She denies the passage time, she denies aging, she denies the reality of "now". Instead, she reconstitutes her life through the perpetual memory of a vague, rosy past. While her cousin Nenè, who was more or less her age, could not bear to live without some hook into the future, Grandmother hesitated and stalled for time, preferring the past. (Bianchini, 172) Bianchini describes Grandmother through the filter of the girl's memory as being unconstrained by time:

> "She did not look like a Grandmother, but like a girl who was getting ready for a ball. She always dressed in pastel colours and wore white felt hats with the brim a little raised on one side. She wore those felt hats in winter and in summer. She did not like the rather clumsy straw hats worn by women of her age very much, because she said that they made her look old. All in all, she dressed in an ageless way: blouses, sweaters, jabots, an umbrella with a silver handle in the shape of an animal's head and her splendid fur" (Bianchini, 104).

It comes almost as a shock, therefore, to discover that Grandmother does suffer the insults of time after all. In a most poignant scene, Bianchini describes how the girl attempts to remember the timelessness of Grandmother by literally putting herself in the older lady's shoes, because, as she justifies to herself, the shoes were almost new and were in style. The shoemaker, who has no emotional commitment to the memory of Grandmother, presents a different reality. In his compliment that the shoes were beautiful, and that "nowadays they don't make them like this any longer. Once people really cared for their shoes" is couched the harsh acceptance that Grandmother had always been subject to the ravages of time (Bianchini, 102). While for the girl, the shoes were a lovely memory of Grandmother, for the shoemaker they were old-fashioned, albeit well-made. The girl has no choice but to accept this weakness in Grandmother, and later admits, in another memory, that Grandmother did belong to another time. As they drink a straight whiskey together for the first time, the girl realizes how unusual that drink was for her Grandmother who ostensibly belonged to "the era of vermouth, at most of martinis" (Bianchini, 139).

There is one more occasion on which the girl feels herself united to her Grandmother by means of a mutually shared object, now belonging to memory. The object is Enzo; he remains an objectified character, never a person in his own right, seen only as the lover of Grandmother and the vicarious lover of the protagonist, who called out

his name in her moments of self-pleasuring. Only one is
the opportunity to bring Enzo into reality of the present,
but the girl lacks the courage to do so:

> "If only she had the courage to speak to Grandmother, to ask
> her: Enzo, a part of our life, yours and mine, where is he? Is he
> dead only for us or for everybody? Or alive only for you and
> me? Why don't you tell me, now that we are alone, and we re-
> member the same things and have the same
> thoughts?" (Bianchini, 174).

The opportunity passes unsatisfied, and Enzo is forever
relegated to memory. Instead, it is precisely at the moment of this crucial missed opportunity that the
protagonist begins to feel strange, and intuits the beginning of her labor (Bianchini, 174). This is a fundamental
moment which neo-psychoanalytic scholar and literary
critic, J. Brooks Bouson, discusses in her work on the relationship between the reader and the 'text of life'. Bouson
suggests that in the text of life of an Other, the reader seeks
to find "some urge by which to live, some basic excellence
or wholeness that links 'acts' to 'need' in an embodied, or
'empathic', mode of awareness." She continues, that "the
act of studying lives is itself a response to the need for
wholeness amidst fragmentation, in which the continuity
of generations is implicit." [2] She describes precisely the situation of *The Girl in Black* for the protagonist is, and
always has been, an admiring reader of the text of her
Grandmother's life, seeking to derive from it some affini-
ties with and some meaning to her own life. She is a reader
who has found in Enzo the point of oneness with her
Grandmother's life text. If she shares those memories with
Grandmother, if she merges into her Grandmother's
memories, then, like the elderly lady, she too will be able
to live only in the past, forever remembering Enzo, forever
sifting through fragments of the past and unable to cope
with the present. But such is not the destiny of the girl.
The imminent birth of her daughter propels her forward
instead, and assures a future for her. For Grandmother,
there is no more future.

Another scholar, psychoanalyst Heinz Kohut, sees in
texts of life, the acceptance of the intergenerational bond of
families, which represents, not merely the stories of famil-

ial conflict (the Oedipus myth), but also of a desire for the future (as exemplified by the myth of Odysseus and his son).[3] His observations, too, are valid for *The Girl in Black*. It is with the birth of Prisca, in fact, that the attitude of the protagonist changes from one of looking always back, to one of accepting a future. Even her bedroom mirror is complicit in this; no longer does it reflect the images of herself that she was used to seeing in the past. Her reflection now, she says, is out of focus . The girl realizes that with the birth of her daughter, she has become another person. (Bianchini, 178). Her reality now is only the unforgiving heat of August that seemed to be almost a punishment from God, threatening to the baby, who unlike Moses, was unlikely to be spared (Bianchini, 180.). Slowly, however, the girl begins to remember her own childhood, and how, in similar bleak circumstances, she had thrived, and survived:

> But for her, when she was a child, there had been no torrid seasons: they were all mild, temperate seasons. She would trustingly put her hand into Mother's hand and enter the shallow water of beaches that were very large, clear and clean, and which might be in America or in Italy. Her mother was young, and often alone. Her mother was also pretty. Sometimes she was deep in thought (Bianchini, 181).

In their imprecision and vagueness, her memories have rendered her childhood a beautiful, safe one, filled with love even in the absence of a father. Suddenly aware of this attitude, the girl is able to reject the dire premonitions of her mother. "why cancel the clear beaches, the fresh June mornings of their brief season of happiness? After all her mother had also been a girl or at least a young woman with a daughter, as happy as she was about Prisca". She begins to feed her child, in a symbolic gesture of life giving. And she realizes that now she can manage on her own (Bianchini, 182). In this realization, the girl is aware of her bond with her mother who, while watching her daughter breast feed her new baby in humble acceptance of the future, remembers how she had done the same many years before. And significantly, it is precisely at this moment, when the girl accepts that there is a future for her and her baby, that we learn of Grandmother's illness and subsequent death. In death, Grandmother, who had lived only in her memories of herself, "[l]ying down, in her rest, became very young again, with an unlined skin, a fresh face, as she had been at the time of her great departures with Enzo. And she left just as the girl had feared she would leave ever since her childhood: forever" (Bianchini, 185).

For the most part, Bianchini's novel is propelled by memory. But in the final chapters, the new attitude brought about by Prisca's birth imposes itself, and the girl begins to seek hope and love in her life. She finally understands, that in positive and negative aspects, she is the continuation of the women of her family; she is the memory of both her Grandmother and her Mother, but she is also herself, and finally she is the anticipation of the future of her daughter. She becomes aware that while the past and the present are completely intertwined, they are, nevertheless, not the same. The realization that the past could never be brought back changes her relationship with Mother. Both of them now focus on the future, represented by Prisca who symbolically "from her stroller, looked at her and called to her with trust and persistence and who stretched her hands towards the walls, the grass and the children" (Bianchini, 209).

With her new anticipation of the future, the girl becomes as all girls, hopefully awaiting the spring. At first she feels as if she were an anomaly, but with the help of the young salesclerk in the clothing store who convinces her to buy new, youthful clothes, the girl renews herself. As the last snow of the year falls around her, she remembers Grandmother, but then loses the reminiscence. Instead, it is the future that is now more important, not the past but the anticipation: "Prisca, on the other hand, needed a dress: she was a child, she was big by now. And the girl was already imagining Prisca's round knees peeking out below the hem. " (Bianchini, 219). The last image, of growth and renewal, contains no old memories, not of Grandmother, not of Mother, not even of the girl in black.

In conclusion, just a brief note regarding the translating of this novel of memories. Memories, as we know, belong to a realm of vagueness, of fuzzy boundaries where time and space overlap. In both English and Italian the imperfect tense is the preferred tense of memory. Unlike the perfect tenses which specify what happened in one moment of time, the imperfect expands to fill time with descriptions of people, places, emotions. The imperfect tense predominates in the original version of the novel, complemented by the sometimes long and winding sentences, imbedded with subordinate clauses, allowed by Italian syntax. This is much closer to the way memory functions. In the English, it has sometimes been difficult to render the same imprecision and meandering of phrase, simply because the English language often refuses this kind of syntax. Nonetheless, the dream-like quality of the girl's reminiscences, the lack of chronological development in the novel, the forfeit of plot for reflection and recollection, do not suffer because of the English insistence on sentences of shorter length, fewer compound and subordinate constructions, or an imperfect tense that is not synthetic, as it is in Italian, but rather composed of the verb "to be" and a gerund. Perhaps the greatest stumbling block will be the imprecision in the description of the character of the girl, who in the Italian version is not hampered by her lack of a name; the English would prefer a much more clearly delineated character, one who is specifically named. On the other hand, Bianchini's *The Girl in Black* speaks to our universal longing to find ourselves through our memories, through the amorphous stories we tell ourselves, through our personal life review of the precise moments that make us who we are today. In this the English translation is true to the original.

Anne Urbancic

Work Cited

Bianchini, Angela. *Capo d'Europa e altre storie*. Milano: Bompiani, 1992.

Hampl, P. *I Could Tell You Stories*. New York and London: W.W. Norton, 1999.

Hutch. R. A. *The Meaning of Lives. Biography, Autobiography and the Spiritual Quest*. London and Washington: Cassell, 1997.

Webster J. D. and B. K. Haight. "Memory Lane Milestones: Progress in Reminiscence Definition and Classification" in *The Art and Science of Reminiscing. Theory, Research, Methods and Applications*, ed. by Barbara

K. Haight and Jeffrey D. Webster. Washington, DC: Taylor and Francis, 1995, pp. 273-86.

Notes

1. Curiously, they are never presented as wives.
2. Hutch, 92.
3. *Ibid.* 93.

The Girl in Black

CHAPTER 1

During the autumn, when Prisca was just over three months old, the girl went to live on her own: that is on her own with her daughter, who in fact was named Prisca. She found an apartment situated between the Celio and the Colosseo and bought it with Grandmother's money: it was a working-class building, situated in a street crowded with shops. In the background, however, there was a very ancient church. From the church's apse and stained-glass window, at sunset, came a strange luminosity that spread to the whole street. The girl's mother did not oppose her decision, she only pointed out that from then on it would take her half a day to come and see Prisca. As a matter of fact, though she said nothing, the girl too was not convinced that she was doing the right thing by going to live at the other end of Rome. Before having Prisca, she had left home three or four times, moving to various locations, in a rather senseless way, if she thought it over now: Trastevere, Piazza Navona, even the Casilina. But these had always been makeshift arrangements, furnished apartments, temporary moves, with girlfriends, and once, for a short time, with a boy. Now, on the other hand, that she was responsible for her child, the move to the Colosseo actually gave her the impression of emigrating to another continent.

"Couldn't you find an apartment in the neighbourhood?" asked Mother.

"In the Parioli district? Certainly not. I can't stand it".

She meant she couldn't stand the porter, the courtyard, the faces and the greetings of the people in the condominium. Every face, every stone was by now used and polished by the years that she had spent in those streets, by the numberless encounters, greetings, by the recurring Christmases, summers, high-school certificates and degrees. One way or another, even with some absences, she had spent a life in that house. In fact, it was her life, twenty-five years.

Above all she could not stand being near Grandmother's empty apartment. Her mother spoke about the apartment every day at the dinner table: wondering whether to sell it, whether to rent it, whether to leave it the way it was: it was impossible to forget it.

And then there was the problem of the furniture.

"So you are going to take the chest?"

"No" said the girl. "No, no".

"Why not?"

"Because I don't like it".

"And to think that you used to say you liked it so much. If you wish, you could leave it with me for a while. It's better than selling it."

"I told you I don't want it. Do as you please".

"What kind of behaviour is this?" said her mother. "Of course it's easy for you not to give a damn about anything".

In the end she took the chest and placed it in one of the two large rooms that, together with the kitchen and the bathroom, made up the whole of the apartment: on a second floor so low that if you leaned out, you could see only the heads of the passers-by and the roofs of the cars. However, thanks to her view, the girl managed to feel in the midst of things and not so isolated as might have happened had her windows instead overlooked the sad entrance, decorated with dark green plants, and the many staircases (staircase A, staircase B) which departed in various directions.

In the other space, the girl organized Prisca's room. The little bed, the changing table and a small chest of drawers looked rather lost but gave the impression of a real children's room, in a real apartment, belonging to a solid family. This cheered the girl up in the evenings, when she found herself alone and came to see how the child was sleeping.

Almost immediately after the move, she enrolled Prisca in the Daycare, which in that district was called Maternity School, or to be more precise, Centre for Newborns and Toddlers. It was situated in an old building which was chipped and crumbling because it had never been painted since the Fascist period. But it was clean and comfortable inside, and had a courteous and efficient staff. Nobody asked her about Prisca's surname, which of course was Luigi's surname. Nobody was interested or enquired about the fact that Prisca was the daughter of unmarried parents. It was a commonplace story, a story that now was no longer noteworthy, less interesting, in a certain way, than the story of her Mother, who had come back from America after her divorce, with her as a three year old child.

She and her mother had a child at exactly the same age, that is when they were twenty-four and a half years old. After her definitive return from America, her mother, however, had taken an apartment in the same courtyard as Grandmother. There was also a cleaning lady named Cesira. Cesira was very nice, always cheerful and always laughing. When she was a child, she went out with Cesira every afternoon, and they often went to the Zoo which Cesira called the Zolò. Cesira was cheerful and good; when she

died, the girl was in grade twelve and Cesira had retired to her village a few years before. Cesira liked to
make fun of foreigners who asked for information in
the street. At that time there were so many Americans.

"They are really funny." said Cesira. "When you
arrived, both you and your Mother used to wear
large dresses that came down to your feet. You made
me laugh so much".

Cesira told the girl that she should not take of-
fence at her words even if she was American.
Actually, the girl was only half American because her
father was an officer in Italy and her mother had met
him after the war. He was a good-looking man, as
was clear from the few snapshots taken in America.
Prisca had completed her elementary education at
the American School in Rome, because of an agreement between her parents. Afterwards they both
must have forgotten that agreement, and so she had
continued her education in Italian schools.

Her childhood had been full of her mother's
friends, whom she called indiscriminately uncles
and aunts, because it was fashionable at the time.
Now that was no longer the custom. So Prisca would
have had no one she could call uncle, because she,
the girl, was an only child, and her mother and
Giovanni had no more children.

She had learnt that her mother was about to re-
marry, while she was at her Grandmother's where
she often went for breakfast.

"By the way" Grandmother had told her that
day, "your Mother is going to marry that dentist who
always comes to your place to play bridge".

They were eating breaded cutlets with fried pota-
toes, one of the foods she liked best, almost as much
as zucchini and ice cream. After all those years, she

still remembered how the breading separated itself from the slightly pink meat. From that time on she no longer ate cutlets. She had said:

"I don't care. After all I will continue to come and see you".

"Of course" Grandmother answered. "Nothing will change. I, for one, will continue going to my own dentist, I don't trust this man at all. Never mind, if mine is a bit expensive: teeth are precious. Leave the meat, if you are not hungry, there is a new flavour of ice cream that you've never tasted".

They had no longer talked about Mother. At one point, with a sigh, Grandmother had said only:

"At least, she will no longer say that she is so lonely".

Instead Mother continued to feel very lonely and to drag Giovanni, who was completely ineffectual, here and there, to theatres, concerts and on trips which he endured in silence, without any comments. Her mother was a very tormented person, even if she was convinced that she was a miracle of equilibrium.

When Prisca was a child, there were plenty of sadistic ladies who enjoyed asking:

"Is it true that the girl's father is not here?"

Cesira managed excellently.

"He's in America" she answered, with a big gesture which included the Ocean, unexplored lands and who knows what else. In this way she silenced them. Mother, instead, if she was present, felt badly about it and offered various anxious explanations; the child's father visited often and was very affectionate. Then, in the street, when they were alone, she tried to remedy:

"There are many children who don't have a father, not everybody has a father; I, for example, lost my father. He died when I was even younger than you are. Then there are those fathers who have to be absent on account of their work, many times men have dangerous jobs, far away from home. It's the women who stay at home, not the men. I'm sure that this summer your father will come to Italy to see you".

It was not true at all. He never came nor had he ever intended to come and, perhaps, if he had really arrived, Mother would have had a terrible crisis. The fact is that with the help of Cesira and her Grandmother the child had managed very well even without her father.

The girl left Prisca at the Daycare and picked her up in the afternoon, around four, but it seemed later to her, because the days were getting shorter and it got darker earlier. Actually, on afternoons when she was freed from her duties at her school which was way at the other end of Rome, and there were neither faculty meetings nor anything else, she would gladly have taken Prisca home a little earlier. She would have liked to look at her again in the light of day, to see whether she had really grown, as the daycare assistants said, and to see, especially, what kind of little face she had.

At times, after teaching her lessons, she strangely forgot to worry about Prisca, and even about herself, about being alone and about the fact that Luigi was far away and that she lived in a strange area. At those times all of a sudden, she felt she could not even remember how big her child was or what she looked like. After so many hours of work, she saw her larger or smaller. Realizing this, she was very shaken by it. She would have liked to take the child back immediately, but after the first few days she realized that at the Daycare Centre they did not like changes in timetable. They told her they wanted to be informed of any changes and informed well in advance. She let it go at that, but she could not help thinking that from the time Prisca was born, her life was full of advance notices and plans: not only for the Daycare Centre, but also for her mother who wanted to plan her visits in advance. In addition she had to stock up on diapers and baby food incredibly early. Even her neighbours, including Anna who had been Grandmother's nurse and had suggested the house near the Colosseo, did not want to be called on to babysit at the last minute, if she had to go out to buy something.

Other people's lives, especially in her block of flats, were full and carefully planned, so that unforeseen events were not allowed. The street was crowded with shops, there was even a kind of little theatre painted in yellow and green and run by feminists. But the girl had already experienced that type of companionship and activity in previous years, and the events of the latest year had detached her from all that: the encounter with Luigi, the pregnancy, Prisca's birth and Grandmother's death.

It seemed to her that her life had acquired a completely different form from that of other girls her age: bursting to the full with chores and duties during the hours when she was with Prisca in the morning and in the afternoon and in the evening. Little by little, day by day, there emerged before her an unforeseen challenge, barely felt when her mother phoned to ask about the child. It was the challenge of keeping Prisca in good health, of making her grow, eat, gain weight: she was the only one who really saw the results, the only one who knew the difficulties, the satisfactions, the defeats. These competing worries took up all her time, and sometimes it seemed to her that they created a kind of second life for her. She wondered whether this happened to all women, and whether the intensity of the commitment depended on the fact that she had to manage everything by herself, or whether this was due perhaps to her particular nature.

And since this commitment was strong and agonizing, it contrasted with the quality of the other hours, those in which Prisca slept or simply did not need her. In those hours she felt the void in her life, even its darkness, as she sometimes thought; a void barely interrupted by Luigi's phone calls. He was always somewhere else, but insisted that he wanted her to understand her that, in spite of this, he was always present. In the course of his phone calls, his words took the form of hurried hammering: he asked about Prisca, about her, but practically allowed no answer. He wanted only to hear her say that she and Prisca were both doing well and to confirm this for himself.

It was quite difficult to explain to her mother and even to the women of her generation Luigi's personality and the necessity of reading between the lines of his conversations. So, the girl avoided speaking about Luigi and her relationship with him.

She lived, therefore, in a kind of isolation which reminded her of her years at the American School, when she pretended to be exactly like the other girls, with bangs, straight shiny hair, short white socks, all pulled up. She pretended she had two American parents, temporarily stationed in Italy. Most of all she pretended to have passing and ironic ties with Italy.

In reality, the only person with whom she could share this repeated rejection of Italy, Cesira and Grandmother, was another child, a half-breed like her. He was the only child of an American father, absent like hers, and of an Italian mother who had never remarried. During school hours, when everyone was busy surviving the cruel rituals of childhood competitions, chats and games, she and Davy never talked to each other. They even avoided looking at each other so as not to betray their defeats and their anxieties. On the bus home from school, at the same hour when she now picked Prisca up from the Daycare, they were brought together by tiredness. Once the real Americans from the Embassies or the FAO (Food and Agricultural Organization) were off the bus, Davy would slide cautiously from his seat to go speak to the driver in Italian or he would place himself in the seat next to him. Then, in the horrible Parioli square, near the newspaper stand, Cesira and the other cleaning lady were waiting for them. They were ready to tidy them up, to button their jackets and coats, making reentry into the other half of their existence easier.

But now the families in her building knew little about her and they had no reason to speak to her about her life. They talked in a cordial, but nervous and cautious way only about children, shopping and television. Even Anna, Grandmother's nurse, who only a short while before, when she was watching over Grandmother, seemed to have understood or guessed everything about their family relationships, here, in the Colosseo district where she lived, had become aloof like the other neighbours. When she stuck her head inside the apartment, to ask about Prisca, she was always in a hurry and, if she stayed for a bit, she was embarrassed and had little to say. However she had recognized Grandmother's armchair:

"Ah" she said "you took it. You did the right thing".

They were both silent for a moment. Then Anna explained:

"Of course, it is a memento".

Above all, the girl had taken the armchair with her so as not to leave it alone: she did not want the armchair to feel that everything was completely over.

What no one knew was that out of all Grandmother's things, besides the fur coat that she did not wear but whose violet perfume she liked to inhale, she had saved a pair of suede shoes, with laces and high heels, fashionable when she was a child. They were almost new, with the heels only slightly worn. Those she had seen on Grandmother must have been another pair, very similar, if not identical to these. She had told herself that they were fashionable again and that she would wear them. For a long time she did not dare to, and anyhow it was not the right season. But when October was over, during one of the first rainy days of November, she went to the cobbler, who turned them over in his hands for a long time, examining them.

"Beautiful shoes" he said. "Nowadays they don't make them like this any longer. Once people really cared for their shoes".

The girl did not tell him that when she had gone with Grandmother to the cubby-hole of the shoemaker, in Via Sistina, she was impressed by two things. She was struck by the long time that Grandmother, who was usually quick, had spent choosing the shape and leather of her shoes and by the sight of the wooden lasts, large and hard, that the shoemaker kept on his shelves and which were the model of Grandmother's small feet.

"All right" said the cobbler, "I shall fix them up. A quick job. Come back in two hours".

He took the piece of leather on which he was working and started cutting it up, with concentration. When she came out, her ears rang with the very

sweet, almost human sound of the leather being cut
by the pressure of the cobbler's knife.

CHAPTER 2

One day, many years before, in her childhood, the girl had taken the key and gone up to Grandmother's apartment. Grandmother's key was to be used only in emergencies and her mother did not approve of her taking it without permission. As for Grandmother, it was not clear whether she might approve or not.

"Certainly" she had said smiling, "it can be useful if I am alone at home and I have a stroke, or, to be optimistic, if I fall and break my hip".

That afternoon her mother was not in. She could not stand her homework any longer and took the famous key. She did not ring the bell. Slowly she turned the key in the lock, opened the door and found herself in the dark hall. The living room was dark and empty, with a single lamp lit up near the sofa. But in the silence, she heard a strange, different sound, a very sweet mewing which came from the end of the apartment. She had never heard it before, and yet she recognized it. It was not Grandmother, and yet at the same time she understood that it was Grandmother. Then, very softly, she closed the door behind her.

At home Mother, who had come back in the meantime, accosted her:

"You know that you must not go up to Grandmother's without telling me".

On her way back Mother had seen Enzo's car parked in the street near the gate.

Every spring Grandmother left with Enzo for one of her trips. At the end of May it hardly ever rained. At the edges of the courtyard hydrangeas blossomed, large and solid, in all the possible shades, from white, to pink to lilac. They were the porter's pride and joy. Sometimes, if it rained, the porter standing by the gate with his wife near him, would greet Grandmother and say:

"Water is good for them. They drink it. You'll see what fine weather we will have tomorrow, Madam".

Grandmother nodded, trusting his words that the rain would stop the next day and the following days. She stood in the middle of the courtyard in a two piece suit, her travelling clothes, and held her, the little grandchild, by the hand. Grandmother, thanks to her elegance and her bearing, enjoyed the approval of the whole building even if, as was clear even then, she led a very different life from the ladies of her age.

She had a very beautiful face, with clear, transparent skin and a sweet, romantic, oval face that was never really sad and that on the eve of her departures with Enzo acquired a dazzling expression. She did not look like a Grandmother, but like a girl who was getting ready for a ball. She always dressed in pastel colours and wore white felt hats with the brim a little raised on one side. She wore those felt hats in winter and in summer. She did not like very much the rather clumsy straw hats worn by women of her age, because she said that they made her look old. All in all, she dressed in an ageless way: blouses, sweaters, jabots, an umbrella with a silver handle in the shape of an animal's head and her splendid fur.

The girl walked slowly towards the Palatino, to while away the time and then go back to the cobbler and to Prisca. She remembered how Grandmother used to say: "And so, my darling, be good and cheerful. We shall meet again very soon. Go out, get some fresh air".

Grandmother did not have clear ideas as far as the girl's studies were concerned. She was always convinced that studying would damage one's health. And then she was sorry to go away and leave her in the city. She stroked her cheek with the palm of her hand, lingering with tenderness. The child felt in her gesture and in her eyes messages of understanding and these gave her comfort.

"Sweetie" said Grandmother once more. "Keep well. I am coming back soon".

She nodded with her head, but the fifteen, twenty days of the trip opened up in front of her like an abyss. Even at that young age she was surprised that what Grandmother considered happiness (which she did not begrudge her), for her could only be cause for loneliness.

She knew very well that Grandmother used to leave with Enzo. Sometimes he even came to fetch her by car. But the child also saw him during the year, when they went out together or when he came up to the apartment to visit. They all knew him: the porters, Cesira, the cook, even Mother, who, however, never spoke of him. If she met him, she gave him a quick greeting that was even more rude than the greeting she gave some neighbours.

"So" said Grandmother, "Is everything ready? My travelling bag? My plaid blanket? Heavens, all that clutter. I am sorry. So much luggage just for a few days".

But the days were not so few. Officially she went to a spa for the waters. And she smiled at everybody, asking to be excused for the inconvenience she caused. But for the girl there had been a special smile right up to the last minute.

"Darling, I am going to send you some postcards. Give me a kiss".

While the cab, or Enzo's car, disappeared down the street, the window framed Grandmother's white hat. It was a proud hat, with a coquettish look, even in the distance. The group broke apart, the porters withdrew, the cook went up to tidy the apartment.

"Come now" said Cesira. "Otherwise, what are we going to eat for lunch?"

"It is a little too cold for the season" said Giovanni at the table, "but the weather will now become beautiful".

Or:

"Did Grandmother's departure go well? Let's hope that the waters will help her knee".

On the day Grandmother left, her mother was in a terrible mood. She was out of sorts from early morning, making a thousand phone calls and planning things aloud in an outburst of crazy activity. She, the child, instead, did not open her mouth, did not make her thoughts known.

Then, thought the girl, the cards started to come, some for the family, many just for her. They said: "I am on my way back" "Kisses from Grandmother", or "From your Grandmother". If they were addressed to her, Enzo almost always signed them as well. She used to meditate on those cards, on the landscapes which formed the background of Grandmother's holidays. There were the Alps, or islands, or cities. There was no trace of health spas.

She crossed the whole of Colosseo Square: nothing disturbed the sleepiness of a dazzling green autumn. She had not been at the Palatino for years. Once she had visited it with Grandmother, during one of those expeditions which in her memory she could not place in a definite year, nor even in the morning or in the afternoon. These were days snatched from the monotony of childhood, always full of sun, surprises and discoveries, expeditions towards enchanted islands where the separation from the land was more important than the uncertain landing.

She rediscovered the smell of damp earth among the marble, the acanthus leaves indented like women's blouses, other leaves which were also green and shiny with an obstinate strength in spite of the season's scant light. They do not know winter is coming, thought the girl. And it will be the end; they will wither and die. The marble of the pillars sank into the dark earth, in the shadowy corners it was cold, but in the sun one felt the desire to soak up the warmth like the little lizards.

One year Grandmother did not leave. During that year Enzo no longer came to visit her. He never came again. On Sundays, when all the others went to Mass, Grandmother no longer got into Enzo's convertible. Little by little she became an old lady. Maybe Enzo had died or was somewhere else. Grandmother never spoke about him and now had gone away with her secret.

I am alone, thought the girl, really alone, in spite of Prisca's existence. Enzo and Grandmother have gone and Luigi cannot be reached. There is no longer the possibility of any contact.

CHAPTER 3

During the autumn evenings, in the apartment at the Colosseo, the girl thought that among the things that belonged only to her, which she kept close - just as she had kept Prisca close to her under her wolf-skin jacket the winter when she was pregnant - there was the fact of Prisca's birth. She was not born at the end of July, as everybody believed and as her birth certificate declared. She was born, or at least the idea of having her was born, almost a year before, in Villa Borghese, on a November day.

She had never told anyone. Only to Grandmother would she have liked to reveal this and many other things. Throughout the whole of her pregnancy she had thought of going to Grandmother and of talking to her as she used to do as a child. But she had always postponed it. Then Grandmother had fallen ill and it had been too late.

It was a November morning. The girl was walking with difficulty. She felt as if at every step she had to cut through a foreign element, which was impassable, or make her way through an invisible obstacle. Instead there was only the fog, that had suddenly descended in the night, the first fog of the year after a golden October. Light and whitish, it softened away the contours of the holm oaks and even of the pines, beyond the gate of the Deer Park. Cars passed cautiously. You couldn't hear their noise and then suddenly they were nearby, with their headlights on. They, too, were trying to create a passage, an opening in the world. The suspended atmosphere and the soggy dampness all around created a dreamlike space, with a destination that was further and further away.

All of a sudden she thought of the possibility of not going anywhere. She could erase the black signs, all stupid and useless, on the white page of her imaginary notebook. As a matter of fact she did not have a notebook. She kept everything in her head: appointments, articles, supply teaching, people to see, phone calls to make, and sometimes she was so full that she felt that her brain would explode. But now she could tell herself: "This morning is mine, the fog is mine, and mine is the act of remaining alone, even if I am not really cheerful". It was an old recurring temptation, but on that day it was accompanied by a feeling of physical weariness that seemed unknown to her, and yet worked silently within her. So all of a sudden she made up her mind

She parked the car near the gate. On the carseat she left, in an untidy leap, the books and papers, the chains of her slavery to those empty, anxious hours which she had been spending for years. Hours which every evening amounted only to a heavy day, without a simple carefree moment. She locked the door and, slowly, as if she was carrying something fragile to be handled with great care, almost a part of herself with which she had not been in touch for a long time, she proceeded along the gate. Now there was a deep silence. The fog had not lifted, in fact it had become thicker, and the cars had almost stopped passing. Out of the whiteness there appeared only parked cars and the silent and locked up villas on the other side of the street. She was alone.

For years she had hardly ever gone to Villa Borghese. Crossing the park, she looked at it without seeing it. The walks taken to Villa Borghese when she was a child were over. And finished were also the walks she took with Sergio, as an adolescent, during holidays and strikes. Every season had its particular corners, areas, trees and trunks, whose colour and feel she could still recall. She could have drawn the map of those areas without mistaking an alley or forgetting a fountain.

The road was now deserted, the traffic noises had died down. Noone passed any longer in that uninhabited world. She arrived at the big gate and slipped into the alley. Under her shoes, she felt the awkward crunching of the pebbles. She looked: there were acorns mingled with the pebbles. Acorns, pebbles, brown earth: it was like having them in her hands and passing them from one side to the other, playing with them. The silence was complete. Hers was a strange return. To the left, now invisible, were the stables with their pungent smell of hay and horses, which the dampness of the morning brought very near. On the other side there were the rows of holm oaks, which usually changed in formation and perspective as one approached them; now they were only large shadows, which loomed darker in the great reign of silence.

In the background, framed by the hedges of the wood, was Venus, the beautiful white statue in the centre of the basin, which in turn was the centre of the Italian garden in front of the Museum. Bent over with the gesture of clasping the drapery to her pubis, she was visible even from the entrance, with her back slightly curved, revealed only down to her hips. The nape of the neck was gently bowed and sweet and soft marble curls played on her neck. She was perfect, like everything else in the Italian garden: the geometric and symmetrical design of the flower beds, surrounded by the small and regular woods, varied according to the seasons: now there were violets, gillyflowers, carnations, and unknown flowers in carpets decorated with arabesques. Against each flower bed, white sarcophagi were set diagonally, slightly smoothed by time, with reliefs that lacked precision. There were also griffins without wings and other statues which were mutilated or snub-nosed but always white and erect, men and women no longer whole, but showing an ancient perfection, whose missing arm or cut off foot or even broken nose coincided with the neglect of the garden.

In the centre of the basin rose tall green leaves, probably papyri, which partially covered the nakedness of Venus. Exotic and familiar, like everything there, they presided over the gentle traffic of boats which rocked gracefully over the almost still water. There too, like everywhere else in the garden, movement was only apparent. In the basin, which was not even large, the boats were all of painted wood, with modest cotton sails and no motors. They remained there, locked, balancing softly on the water, wedged against the water lilies. And yet under the gaze of the children who leaned anxiously at the edges, there had never been a more real boat traffic than that one, never more longed for departures, never a stretch of water which offered a comparable emotion. At any rate, all that she saw again as she walked around, was naturally invisible. This happened not only because the landscape was hidden by the fog, which unravelled here and there, only to close again, with its white and penetrating dampness, but also because she saw that landscape inside herself, as if she had stored it during all the years spent elsewhere; as if she had passed many other times in front of the statues with cut off arms and empty eye sockets.

When she arrived inside the enclosure of the Italian garden, she was forced to realize that everything was different: the wooden benches painted green were splintered, some even broken and missing almost all their planks, and in the basin there were no longer water lilies, only dirty bits of paper floating on top and even more of them lying on the bottom. The bottom of the basin, that once could be seen through the transparent, magic water that rocked the little boats, now revealed cracks and chaps beneath the dirty greenish water. In place of the flowerbeds, where the violets had twisted in many coloured arabesques, only a little grass shrivelled by the cold survived.

Instead there survived the design of the garden, like an indelible trace or thought of the person who had originally planned it. It survived with obstinacy. They could render it vulgar, they could dirty it and neglect the borders of the dwarf box-trees that lined it. And yet, in spite of the broken statues, which instead of arms showed the piece of iron that had supported the marble, that wonderful design, which had seemed to her the first image of the world's harmony, continued to survive.

It seemed as if something was about to happen, but in reality there was nothing that could happen. It was only a morning like all the others, a little bit damper, and for her, a little lonely. An autumn morning, before another winter, before a year that would bring holidays, trips, tours, outings. For two or three hours she did not have to organize anything; nobody was going to look for her. A morning of freedom. But she did not need a morning of freedom, thought the girl suddenly. She needed to feel alive again, as she did once, when she came there with Cesira, when if they spoke to her of Paradise on earth, of the Garden of Eden, she saw this place: the flowerbeds like arabesques, the shining leaves of the lemons, strong in the big vases, the solemn and familiar *façade* of the Museum, with its large windows.

It was at that moment that she fell a strong cramp in her stomach. She found a bench, near a sarcophagus, all wet with hoar-frost, and sat down. She felt a weakness, a tiredness that now weighed also on her lids and drove her to recapture the dream of the morning before it was torn away from her.

She leaned her head against the back of the bench and closed her eyes, forgetting the cold and the dampness for a moment. While her cramps were still light, only brief contractions above the pubic area, the vital centre, she was invaded by a sweet languor, almost a desire to make love. It ran beneath her skin, sometimes stronger, almost painful, other times barely perceptible along her legs, down to her calves and the ankles, like an inner river which melted inside her and fertilized her, making her a little bit sick and weak, but, somehow, more alive. More alive than on other days, when she felt well, when she did not have her period, she thought with her eyelids, getting as heavy as lead. More alive than when she was whole and dry, without this inner ebbing and flowing.

Now she was sitting in a labyrinth of apparitions and of survivors: behind the Museum's windows there were no visitors, only shadows that lingered and disappeared, distorted by the window panes. And there appeared other visions, incongruous, against the light: an arm, a straight head, a knee.

At one point the deep, compact silence was not enough to explain the strangeness of the day. She looked around and understood from where she derived her sense of void. The children were not there. In the Italian garden, neither they nor anyone else was present: it was totally deserted. But she had not seen them even before, at the entrance or along the alley: the benches were empty, and the great esplanade around the water tank was empty. In the fog only some adults were wandering around, one could hear only the barking of some dogs.

But I am here for the children, thought the girl. I came to look for them. I wanted to see them, how they play, how they move. For the past few months, or perhaps a year, she had been stopping to look at them in the street or in stores. The bigger children in strollers, already grown up, with their serious and severe gaze, that only rarely broke into a smile. The others hidden under blankets, behind curtains: it was always a surprise when they emerged from their prams.

That morning, the children were somewhere else: in the supermarkets, in the kindergartens, in the cars. Now she remembered that people said that no one went to Villa Borghese any longer: there was little time and a great fear of kidnappings. The world of nannies and of servants like Cesira was over. She was there, all by herself, in the damp and inhospitable cold which was starting to penetrate her bones, on that broken bench that hurt her back. The warm and pleasant languor she had felt before was abandoning her little by little. The tide was ebbing gradually and left her on a shore covered with waste paper, plastic bottles, watermelon rinds and other rubble that had dissolved at the bottom of the basin. In vain had she hoped to find the ancient drawings of the sea on the sand, the crunching of the pulverized shells, the salty smell of the sea: in vain had she hoped that the womb, the uterus that had woken up that day, at the same time, as a kind of miracle, would receive her.

At that moment two strange things took place almost at the same time. At the bottom of the garden, to the right of the Museum, the road was flanked by a white banister of griffins and lions, dominated by two curious structures, aviaries, painters' studios,

identified only as places of delight, enchantment
and mystery, with their pinnacles, cupolas in white
iron, with their many and varied decorations, no
longer white, but pink or perhaps the colour of brick,
and their enclosed gardens, a smaller version of the
Museum garden, but even more beautiful, small and
perfect. There, in that place where she had not yet
been and saw everything only in the imagination, a
dark spectre entered the whiteness of the fog. The
black shadow seemed to have two faces. It advanced
slowly, with a way of moving that was not like walking; it had in front of it a smaller shape, that seemed
to possess a head, but stretched out immensely
behind its head, like a camel, so as to render everything absolutely unknown, unreal. It seemed part of
the proteiform changes of the day, part of a dream
that began to come out of the girl and invade her
surroundings. And while she was about to yield to
her tiredness and give up trying to understand, all of
a sudden, a puff of wind took the fog away and transformed everything. Above the trees and the cupolas,
the sky was clear, already wintery but flooded by the
sun. Everything seemed manoeuvred by an impresa-
rio, tired of mystifications.

The strange centaur-like figure entered her field
of vision, in the narrow space of the Italian garden. It
became double: one tall, black spectre with a black
wide-brimmed hat, and a small child, completely
different, in pastel colours, pink, white, blue, sitting
in a basket which leaned against the handlebar. The
camel was then a bicycle, and the black bandit with
the large Calabrian hat was now wheeling it with
one hand, while with the other arm he held the
child.

How strange, thought the girl, how wonderful.
They too are here, like me, in a kind of miracle:
unusual like the morning, like my pause, like my

weariness. They have the determinate, punctual and proteiform quality of dreams. That's why they will disappear, and I already know that I shall not find them ever again. Following them with her gaze, she imagined them crossing the garden, passing among the flower beds devoid of arabesques and the basin whose stagnant water with dark reflections was now revealed by the sun. She imagined them disappearing towards the exit, on the side of the street, into the city, and vanishing for ever. When she felt another cramp, she closed her eyes, mostly out of boredom, but also not to see the end of the apparition. When she opened her eyes, everything was changed once more. After leaving everything else behind her, including the exit and the Museum, the black figure was moving in a diagonal towards her, the only inhabitant of the planet Villa Borghese. When the figure had gone past the basin, she realized it was a girl wearing an old, black, Borsalino hat, which resembled a bandit hat only from afar and a close-fitting, or rather tight velvet jacket, in the style of the forties. The child had a red jumpsuit.

She sat herself down on the bench, next to her. Very rapidly she untied the child from the straps that held him in the basket; then she picked him up as if he were a parcel, a bright red parcel. With the tender strength of her long, shapely hands, without gloves, she held the child under the armpits, while he looked at her intensely.

Finding himself free, the child swayed on his short, red legs, tried to move, tottered even more, and fell in a sitting position on the pebbles. Right in front of them. He did not even seem to want to cry. In fact he smiled with a sweet and cunning air. He looked not at his mother but at the girl, staring with keen interest. He took the hood with his small hands and pulled it back several times until he managed to free his head, as if he wanted to show off. Then she saw that he had smooth, thin, blond hair, which shone clean in the sun. His head had a long shape, a little bit like Davy and the other little boys of the American school; his skin was also light, but his long hair which curled a little on his neck took away his American Marine look.

"You like him" said the girl in black.

She was not asking, she was asserting in a low and rather hoarse voice.

Her voice matched her appearance, even her accent which was slightly affected. She looked at her who, until then, had not turned round, seized by a strange shyness.

Then the girl in black, with a bold gesture, seized her hat by the brim and took it off. The gesture was that of a musketeer, but a mass of raven black hair tumbled down and, parting in the middle, it framed her dark, oval, Mediterranean face.

"Do you like him?" this was a question and might mean anything.

It was, above all, a show, of the type that young girls of today put on all the time. They seem to have always an audience to whom they can address words and gestures in mind. But it was also a dialogue and meant: did you see, I came and sat right next to you, I did not leave you all alone.

She nodded. She liked him as part of the miracle of that day, of that sky that kept clearing up, above them, allowing them to perceive an ever larger space of blue, while the fog gathered at the borders of that kind of lake, turning itself into clouds. The three of them were in the damp and stark garden.

"Marvellous" she said.

"He really is my son, you know, even if he does not look at all like me".

"I imagine so. Certainly".

"Well, he might also not be mine".

"It happens".

"That's true".

She wasn't angry, but spoke quickly: she clearly had to make some statement.

And equally clearly she had to communicate with her, with the girl. This was the important point. That day everything had acquired importance and meaning, just as it happens in dreams. Everything was portentous not only for the present but, much more, for the future. There was a message somewhere. Not to be lost, rather to be found. She felt she had not been speaking for a long time: an activity which appeared to her almost new and to be discovered again. Words rose in silence only to fall down again with a strange sonority, a kind of echo. Each one was detached and yet part of a dialogue that had started elsewhere.

"What do you do?" asked the girl in black rapidly.

She opened her mouth to answer, still in doubt of where to begin: what she did in general, or that particular day. She would not have found it at all difficult to speak of her life in general. But the other person added decisively:

"I mean the important things".

For a minute she was irritated by this hurry and no longer felt open to a dialogue which, after all, had been started by another. Then, following the gaze of the other person, she discovered that she was observing her hand leaning on the lid of the sarcophagus from her side of the bench. One of those sarcophagi which belonged to her childhood, when she believed that throughout the world children played the way she did, on sarcophagi polished by time and bad weather.

In the meantime, the child stood up. And since nobody was paying attention to him, he had been touching the gravel and the damp earth and had smeared the whole of his face. Now, standing on his feet and leaning against the girl's knees, he stared at her. He was within reach of her hand, the other hand.

"What do you do?" repeated the girl in black.

Up to that moment, through her fingertips, she had felt the stone's porosity, the little holes bordered with moss, without realizing it, without becoming aware of it. They were soft to touch: she went over them one by one, like an itinerary, along the wrinkled surface where days, months and years had traced different paths. For the first time she felt that the contact of her hand, looking for its own place or path on the sarcophagus, was connected by an internal rhythm with the languorous weakness that had settled within her from her waist down, in her stomach, as far as her pubis.

"Do you paint?"

"No".

"Do you sculpt?"

"Not at all".

The girl in black was surprised, but no more than she herself had been upon seeing the other appear in the garden. Black figure and inquisition came together: she felt herself investigated and weighed down by the girl in black who would be the one to decide whether to take her or abandon her there.

A majestic cat with a voracious look, emerging from under a hedge of noble myrtle, passed by, followed by two or three others.

"They always come at this time" she announced. "It's those damned cat ladies who spoil them".

"Do you often come here?" she asked tentatively.

She answered in the same dismissive way as before:

"I have to. What else can I do with him?"

He was their third interlocutor. He kept on staring at them or glancing from one to the other, connecting them now with his continuous coming and going. He stooped and took the little pebbles with difficulty, bending his little body, too fat on his legs which were still very short. He seemed to be sighing a little. When he was in front of her, he waited for her to open her hand. He placed his pebbles inside her hand, she smiled, he smiled. She received a subtle joy from his thin, smooth blond down, barely turned up at the tips, which kept peeking out of the hood. His mother had pulled up his hood on his head and he had shaken it back again.

She thought that the dampness might give him a head cold. If she had dared, she would have taken his head between both her hands and with her fingers she would have played with his ears, which were small, well shaped and close to his head. Just as one does with kittens, with a voluptuousness that spreads from the animal to the person who is stroking it. Standing stiffly, without moving, she could already see herself touching that soft skin and she imagined on his face the smile that would light up at her touch.

She wasn't able to see the girl in black. But she felt on her the girl's deep black eyes, which she had briefly glanced at when she had loosened her hair.

She did not know what she looked like, whether she
was beautiful, or, as it had seemed to her, whether
she was somewhat dark, dull and wrinkled. It would
have been indiscreet to turn her head. She had to be
careful.

"You need a child" she told her all of a sudden.

She did not ask her: how did you guess? "Yes"
she answered. Then: "No". Then: "Of course, it's
true. I should have someone close to me. I'm not saying I'm missing something, the others say that. I'm
missing everything".

The wind started blowing and it became a little
cold.

The child continued going back and forth. He
carried pebbles, making little heaps of them and
undoing them, while casting a side glance at his
mother to make sure he was not being watched. Or
maybe that he was being watched. Then he started
again, tottering and unsteady, towards the basin. It
seemed as if his mother wasn't taking any notice of
his trips. But, when he was half way there, she would
stop him with a shout:

"Alec!"

He stopped in his tracks, but if by chance he continued this - and even he understood that it was a
game - and he did not come back, she would get up
and with long legged strides she would catch him
again. Then she would scold him, calling him names
that made him laugh, and she would give him a big
kiss, bringing the very small face of the child to her
mouth level and sucking him in as if he were a fruit.
It was a pantomime, wild and very tender at the
same time.

"Is he American?".

"Him? No. Why?".

"His name".

"Ah, his father liked it". She had looked at her. She had shrugged her shoulders: "He was a nobody. It's the child who matters."

He stopped, stared at them, reversed gear. The girl in black got up, majestic and Spanish looking, took him in her arms and, sitting down again, placed him on one of her knees. Holding the child with one hand, with the other she pulled food wrapped with crumpled pieces of coloured papers, jars of baby food, rolls, cooked ham, processed cheese, out of a knapsack, pressed between her thighs. The girl in black turned out to be an expert at feeding her son. In fact, with her long, aristocratic fingers she managed to unscrew the cap of the thermos while holding the child on her knee. Then, placing the cap under her chin, she took off the stopper, poured the liquid into the cap now transformed into a cup, and made the child drink. Leaning out from his mother's protective arms, he swallowed with small gulps, like a little animal.

"You see" she said, "he's famished".

Then the child began to rub his dirty little hands over his face, his eyes and his ears.

"He's sleepy" she said tentatively.

"Of course. Now we're going home" said the girl in black.

She had to let her go. She was busy, she had a life, commitments. And anyhow, while at Villa Borghese, she had often experienced a feeling of loss in the past. Some afternoons between autumn and winter, when one could smell the pungent odour of leaves burning somewhere in the park and the sun had turned red behind the very tall pine trees of the Parco di Siena, Grandmother used to pass by on foot. Sometimes she was late. Then the girl would abandon her games and go next to Cesira, turning her head continuously towards the end of the park, where Grandmother might still appear. Then Grandmother would arrive. Tall, elegant and tender, she bent to embrace her brushing against her with her fur collar, which gave off a subtle perfume of violets, always the same. They all looked at her. They also looked at the girl, proud and happy. After releasing her from her arms, Grandmother took her by the hand protectively, a gesture she savoured almost with sorrow, because that passage was too brief and that union too transient.

"What a beautiful sunset, don't you think?" Grandmother used to say affably. "My girls, now go back home, for it's already damp. As for me, I walk so fast that I get warm. Bye darling, bye love. See you tomorrow, sweetie".

She would disappear again with her quick step, and her slender, ageless figure, down the alleys which were getting darker, now pierced sideways by the last rays of the sun. She went towards the dramatic dusk, all red or purple, towards the vast city, which lay just outside, beyond the gates, towards a place elsewhere, which for her, as a child, was called Enzo. She felt a fierce and tormenting desire for some paradise to which one day she would have a right.

The girl in black got up, with a determined look. She cleaned Alec's face. He let her do it; his eyes were already half closed. She put his hood back on his head and, efficiently, arranged the food, the knapsack and all the paper wraps in the bike carrier, all the while holding Alec tightly under her arm. The child swayed a little, half asleep.

Somewhat similar to Medusa and to Sybil, the girl in black got on her bike, barely said goodbye with a wave of her hand, and went away with Alec.

She took a different road from the one she had taken at her arrival and she disappeared swiftly into the emptiness out of which she had emerged.

When she started towards the gate, the world was profoundly changed. She raised her eyes to look at the sky: it was a deep blue, as if summer or spring had come back. Or an unknown season with a gentle warmth.

I have to go home, she thought: I can do what I want I can decide for myself. I'm going to put myself at the centre of the world and arrange everything around me.

CHAPTER 4

Two months after that November day at Villa Borghese, she announced to Grandmother:

"I'm going away. I must go away".

"What's happening to you?" asked Grandmother.

She was sitting in an armchair. That afternoon the girl realized that Grandmother almost always sat in an armchair now.

"What's the matter with you, darling? You seem out of breath".

"I ran up the stairs".

"Why didn't you take the elevator?".

Unintentionally Grandmother had guessed. Yes, it was certainly not good for her health to run up the stairs, but the fact was that she was feeling nauseous and, in the elevator, it was even worse. Grandmother had not come to open the door. She realized all of a sudden that this, too, had not happened for quite a while. After the famous cook of Enzo's time had disappeared, because she had retired to her village, there had been a dizzying sequence of housekeepers who went out at all hours or shut themselves in their room to sleep, not very available, in any case, to answer the door. So she had got used to the joy of finding Grandmother's smiling face at the entrance: her very white skin was stretched over her cheekbones which were still full, her hair was all white, carefully combed in waves that had become fashionable again, and her eyes were blue, large and luminous. Upon seeing her granddaughter, she immediately became happy and festive. Then one day, with a hesitant voice, she had told her on the phone: "Take the key please. In case I don't hear the bell or I'm in my room". From that moment, she had used the key, with the old feeling of committing a burglary and of catching Grandmother by surprise. But there had been no more surprises. There was only Grandmother, rarely in her room, almost always stuck in the living-room's hard back armchair. Sometimes she read, with her rather dull glasses, that she took off as soon as she heard her. Other times she knitted, but without any enthusiasm. Or, sometimes, she did nothing. However, she would sit up immediately, in anger: "What a stupid life. What a nuisance to be old".

"I'm going away" the girl repeated.

"When are you coming back?"

"How are you feeling?" and she kissed her lightly.

"What's the matter?" and Grandmother placed one hand in her lap and the other on the arm of the chair. The white sleeves of her sweater were a little worn at the elbows from leaning on the chair for so many hours.

"I am expecting a baby. It will be born in August, at the end of August".

"A baby?" asked Grandmother slowly. "What are you saying? This is a complete surprise!".

"Yes".

"There must be a man".

"Of course".

"What's he like?"

"His name is Luigi".

Having spoken his name in such an awkward way, the girl thought she had already spoilt everything. Hers seemed only another of those endless women's stories with a sad ending. Women would mention the name and then rattle off their story in its entirety with the utmost pleasure, turning the words in their mouth as if they were a sweet candy.

"What does your....friend do?" Grandmother looked for the words.

The girl shuddered, but once more, the right word was not available.

"Anyhow" added Grandmother, "you are a little bit mixed up".

An unpleasant and improvised definition, thought the girl, who felt offended once more.

"It's not true".

She was more mixed up before, when she pretended that all went well and instead everything had gone badly. Now it was different, now she would have a child. She already had a child inside her, her breasts would swell, something was finally happening to her after so many years.

"It will be a very beautiful experience".

"All right. Are you going to get married"?

"I don't know. I don't think so".

"My goodness" sighed Grandmother.

"Are you worried?"

"Heavens" mused Grandmother "can it be that we only ask each other questions?"

The fact was that with Grandmother also, the only person with whom, after all, she could speak, she had to take long and winding roads, choosing and discarding her words, for fear of not being understood.

As a child she did not know how to concentrate:
her mother said that she was absent-minded, in a
daze. At school and out they always talked about her
absent-mindedness. But the simple matter was that
she did not want to reveal herself. She remained
closed up, intent on thinking about her own things,
like a little snail keeping its horns well drawn in.
Now she no longer wanted to be cautious.

"What do you want me to say? I cannot tell you
fibs".

"Of course not".

"We don't know if we're going to get married".

"Is he already married?" Grandmother tried to
speak casually.

The silence that followed seemed full of suspended thoughts and also full of conclusions that
were impossible to draw. And yet, thought the girl,
the great subject between us has always been love. It
was a great axiom, she had been taught by Grandmother in a distant, faraway past, that love was
indeed an important thing, the most important, in
fact the only one for which it was worthwhile to
commit oneself. But not even she, the girl, had managed to understand if Grandmother believed in
marriage only as a rite or how much she stuck to
that faded image of a husband who had died young.
An image which Mother persisted in commemorat-
ing: "Daddy did this. Daddy liked that. Daddy would
not have wanted this. How good Daddy was".
Grandmother managed only to nod courteously,
without feigning sorrow for that premature death:
"You are right. You are quite right".

The girl reacted angrily:

"You are interrogating me. You too. As if mother
weren't going to make enough scenes".

Leaning on the arm of the chair, behind Grandmother, the girl burst into tears. The first outburst
after so many years came as a great relief.

Grandmother interrupted:

"All right, all right. Why are you so desperate?
Why are you crying now? You're telling me you're
pleased to have this baby and you cry? Why make all
this fuss, if everything is all right?"

Things were not quite all right. They were all
right and yet they were not. They both knew it. At
that moment they had somehow found each other,
but had lost Enzo. Grandmother had immediately
understood that Luigi would never be Enzo.The girl
had dreamt about Enzo all her life, ever since she had
found him next to her on a vaguely remembered day
of her childhood. Twenty five years old, with a tuft
of brown hair and very light eyes: he and Grandmother were always together. To see one meant to
expect the other or to be sure that he was not faraway. At every hour he would wait for her in the car
and carry her parcels and, when they left, her suit-
cases. At dinner, in the evening, the cook would
serve them both.

"Aren't you staying with us, darling? Why don't
you eat with us? I am going to phone Mother and tell
her, darling." She would shake her head and go away
with dignity to the long-faced evenings with
Giovanni and her mother. Grandmother and Enzo
would go out: she followed them without jealousy,
except for a little, or rather a lot of sorrow on account
of those too long journeys. But she was comforted by
the thought that he belonged to her just as he
belonged to Grandmother.

Enzo was young, more or less Luigi's age. And
this made everything plausible. And he was nice,
sweet, compliant and considerate in his courtesies,
endowed with the tenderness of those who are

strong. He protected those who were presumed to be weak: her and Grandmother. Grandmother because she was so much older than he was, and her because she was a child. They had to be protected. He seemed to assert this every time he opened the door for them, took heavy things out of their hands, brought them presents. And they felt protected and loved. Both of them, in the same way, even if by different means. The girl got toys, sweets and caresses. How pretty you are, how intelligent you are, did you hear what she said, sing us a song from the American School, tell us about your teacher. This one, when she is older, will make life difficult for you. She is a flirt, that's what she is. He spoke and Grandmother smiled as she listened to him. The child was their masterpiece. At the time Enzo was not wealthy. He had become wealthy later on, a successful architect. On the contrary, he was poor then and came from a humble background, at least in comparison with Grandmother's comfortable life style. But this too was part of his charm. And then he was a man of the world, as Grandmother had guessed very well.

"Why do you complicate life so much" sighed Grandmother.

"Do you think that marriages and divorces are not complicated?"

Grandmother sighed again:

"Certainly, your life has never been easy".

The girl would have liked to answer: yes, of course, even now we keep a very delicate balance and we speak in code. But in fact it had always been like that. A faraway father, in America, whom she had seen only in a photograph, had been less worrying during childhood and adolescence, than a thirty year old Enzo, near her.

She almost felt she was their daughter, which was quite natural since Enzo was so young and Grandmother too seemed so young and beautiful and strong. Sometimes she even imagined that her mother had never existed and that she, the child, was the daughter of that tender friendship to which she was always privy. A mother like Grandmother, a father like Enzo: it would have been divine.

"We do what we can" said the girl.

"Of course" Grandmother's voice sounded surprised "what else can you do?"

All right, the girl would have liked to answer, all right. Then she should have said that she had already managed as best as she could. Not even Grandmother, who loved her so much, had ever suspected. And anyway she was so taken with Enzo, that it seemed quite natural to her and not at all dangerous to include the girl in this love. As for Mother, perhaps she had guessed. Because she was smart and also because her hatred for Enzo gave her a second sight.

"I thought you were happy".

She had the same affectionate and slightly disappointed voice with which she sometimes received her refusal to stay for supper. Why refuse to be happy? As long as she could, she, Grandmother had been happy inside and outside. Happiness was reflected in the splendour of the eyes, in her shining face, in her sweetly tempered voice. Criticisms, sour faces, rancour did not touch her. For her, the child, it had been different. She had had to carry everything inside and use it for her private theatre, where life moved and where her characters acquired body and soul. But everything had happened when she was ten or eleven years old.

"You are beautiful, you are intelligent. People like you. Why are you like this? Why are you desperate?"

Grandmother could not know. During the end of high school and throughout university she had kept out of the way. She visited very little so that Grandmother, who became increasingly older and more lonely, wouldn't realize that her granddaughter was also lonely. Instead, during the times of Enzo and of her childhood, she was always there, always in the house. They were always calling her. People who are happy always need a mirror to reflect their happiness, they need to share with others their surplus of affection and emotions. And she, as a child, had acted as their sounding board. Enzo and Grandmother were at her disposal, attentive, full of flattery: "Look at her, how much she has grown in these few months. In a short while we shall have to think about finding her a husband. What kind of husband do you want, darling? You don't want to get married? But how are you going to manage without a husband?" Enzo, as usual, spoke without restraint, cheerful, playful, enchanting. Grandmother smiled in silence, or said with tenderness: "What nonsense are you putting into her head?"

Had she heard Enzo's obsessions, Mother would have become scandalized. She would have created an eleventh commandment on things that one must not say. Grandmother, instead, liked Enzo just because he entertained her, because he had the ability to make her laugh, to amuse her, to make her dream.

As a ten or eleven year old child she used to go to bed very early, leaving Giovanni and her mother in the living room staring at the television, and Cesira in the kitchen, cleaning the dishes and listening to the radio. Later on also Cesira got her own television and she could be heard laughing by herself.

She pleasured herself every night. Every night the doors of a theatre opened to her. She found Enzo, punctually, every night. There, in the certainty of her loneliness, of her complete separation from the world, her hands became adult and very skilful. Lying on her side, the tips of her thumb and forefinger, exact and very skilful, moved slowly, cautiously, but confidently to touch and penetrate, enough to give her a measured and satsfying pleasure. Then, in that gesture unknown to everyone and which no one could prevent, she triumphally recovered the right to a love that was hers, but, in a miraculous way came also from others, from the outside. In fact in the other arm, bent under her head, she found a person who would encourage her, push her to go a little further, towards a limit that only he knew, but at which she was aware she wanted to arrive. Sometimes in the morning, she found herself in her own arms, always protected by two persons, herself and the other man, who had ferried her through the night and promised her that when she would be a grown up, she would have a much greater happiness of which this was a certain beginning.

"It's all right about the baby" said Grandmother, "Of course, I am very happy about it".

The girl stroked her hand which had veins on the surface and was flecked with liver spots. She had never noticed it before. Hands reveal age even more than wrinkles. Once Grandmother had splendid hands which Enzo kissed lightly upon arriving and upon leaving, or all of a sudden, on an impulse.

When she was sixteen, the girl had met Sergio, who was a drummer and did not look at all like Enzo. But he too made her laugh and tousled her hair. Heaven was in his fingers which played behind her ears, when he took her head between his hands as if she were a kitten. He did not call her "darling", he called her "pussycat".

The theatre was about to open, the show could begin. That summer Sergio was going to Sardegna with his band and wanted her to go along with him. Maybe love would begin there.

It was already May, but that year, between the moment the porter peered at the hydrangeas, still pale and mysterious, and wondered whether they would be pink, white, blue or even lilac and the moment where every flower blossomed, full of beauty, Grandmother did not leave. Nor were there any preparations for a journey. The girl realized it one afternoon, when she heard someone behind her calling her in the street. She and Sergio both turned round. They walked hugging each other, the boy with his arm round the girl and the palm of his open hand embracing her hip, she with the same gesture, but with greater difficulty, because he was taller. She only managed to stick her hand into his jeans' pocket, where she felt under her fingers, at every step, the vibrations of his tight muscles.

"The Italian flag" Enzo had exclaimed.

He had locked the car, almost in front of the house. They had caught up with him, going up the street, always holding each other by the waist. They had looked at each other laughing: it was true. Sergio wore a red jersey and with his blond hair cut in bangs around his head, looked like a page. She wore a white shirt and jeans and a green shawl thrown around her throat and shoulders.

"You are beautiful" Enzo announced.

Instead he appeared older that day, his hair thinning at the temples. He wore an outfit that Grandmother would not have liked, thought the girl. He looked like a wealthy man, a businessman with a boat: a blue shirt and wrapped around his neck a silk scarf. This was the same Enzo who for so many years had only had old clothes and his cheerful youth.

Instinctively she had asked:

"When are you leaving, you and Grandmother?"

"I have no idea" he had answered, "I don't know".

His face had darkened and he had become silent. She, however, had not noticed, and had not asked anything else.

She never saw him again. Ever! Then her mother said no to her trip to Sardegna. The reasons she gave were all motivated by a confused and indefinite fear.

She had not let her go to Sardegna because she was afraid Sergio was a homosexual or a scoundrel, or that he took drugs or that she too took drugs. The matter was never made clear. Mother was also afraid that she would leave school to follow Sergio.

The girl had phoned Grandmother. The cook had left for her village, as she did every year during that season. Grandmother's shutters were almost lowered. Maybe she too had left, thought the girl, maybe she too had gone away with Enzo: "How strange, they did not say anything to me". The phone had been ringing for a long time, as happens in an empty house, as happens now that Grandmother has really gone away. Instead at that time Grandmother had finally answered, but after a long time and with such a changed voice that for a minute she had not recognized her.

"Grandmother, you must help me. I want to leave with Sergio. You must speak with Mother. You must do that for me, Grandmother. Please".

Grandmother had not hesitated, answering in a tired, hoarse voice:

"I can't do it. I can't talk to your mother. You mustn't ask me to. It's impossible. You must solve your own problems and leave me in peace".

She spoke this way, without even saying darling, darling, don't cry, don't get upset. The girl had remained there, with the black phone receiver in her hand, not understanding. She went to look for Sergio, anxious and desperate. But all of a sudden, he couldn't be found, since he was busy in recording studios located in various parts of the city. She and Grandmother had never spoken again of that phone call. As if it had never been made, as if it had occurred in a dream. And she sometimes wondered whether she had really not dreamt that hoarse voice with the incredibly detached tone. Grandmother, who had gone off so many times, now no longer left the apartment; the girl, who had never gone away, was completely confused by her new self, blossoming to love.

One day Grandmother reappeared in the street with her perfect outfit, her wide brimmed panama hat, which that year replaced the bright, wide, youthful felt hats, that she used in winter. She was wearing a very beautiful silk print suit which noone had seen before. The girl heard her in the courtyard satisfying the curiosity of the porters and of the other tenants, in a serious but politely curt tone. "Yes. I haven't been well. But now everything is all right. Thank you, thank you. Have a good summer. Yes, I shall leave later on, for the usual treatment". Only then did she realize that everything had been true. Beneath the large hat, Grandmother's face was ravaged, the proud mouth struggled not to tremble. And the wonderful silk print, all shades of lilac and pink, fell from her thin shoulders and opened on a gaunt decolleté.

The girl, brought suddenly back to the present, asked with trepidation:

"Are you feeling all right, Grandmother?"

"What's the matter with you, darling? You are really agitated. Why are you looking at me that way?"

She had spontaneously juxtaposed the present figure, the lady with the pastel cardigan and the nicely combed snow white hair, with the other figure, the one that had appeared in the courtyard six or seven years before. The lady in the courtyard showed signs of devastation, but also, somehow, signs of the love she had once enjoyed. The rush, the fury were still in her, however aching and tortured. But now no longer; there were only old age and calm. Then, in spite of her height, she fretted about getting fat; now she no longer worried about this. Grandmother had gained a little weight, but she was no longer slender or elastic, she no longer had the narrow waist on which she had shown off the tall, shiny, gaudy belts which were all her pride and joy. As if she did not have the fountain of youth: *fontaine de jouvence*, she called it jokingly. "Don't you know what it is," she said to Enzo, "don't you know at all?" "I'm an ignorant man," he said, "I haven't travelled like you: where is it? This spring that you mention, is it in Florida, in faraway countries?" It was an old joke, one of those that always exist among couples. "No, no," said Grandmother, and she toyed with her fan and tapped him on the wrist, on the fingers: "Not faraway at all. I have a private one, that belongs to me, very close by." They joked without paying attention to her, still a child, without even imagining that she, too, understood, that she too was becoming aware of things.

Once, in the kitchen, she had suddenly understood the notion of liquid of youth: a liquid that, as Cesira and Grandmother's cook said laughing, is good for women's skin. They had not paid any attention to her, but she had stored the fascinating idea and the notion then became part of the great theatre between Grandmother and Enzo.

Now Grandmother no longer had elixir of love; the fountain of youth had dried up.

"What are you thinking, darling?"

The girl blushed.

"What's the matter with you?" insisted Grandmother.

"Nothing".

"Shall we have a whisky?"

She went towards the cabinet where she kept the liqueurs. The interior was lined with red damask and the chandelier cast light on the bottles and the goblets.

"You drink whisky!"

She poured it cautiously, like somebody who is not used to it and considers it only a remedy.

"On doctor's orders" she said rather slowly and slowly she continued pouring a drink into the other glass. "I have it in the evening, at this time".

"In the evening, every evening?"

In her own voice, stupidly repeating Grandmother's sentences, she sensed the dismay for all those lonely evenings of solid, unbroken silence.

"My God, you have become so uptight. Don't make that face at me. The doctor says it's good for me. And then you, young people, don't you always drink?

What do doctors say to well-preserved ladies, who have maintained their youth beyond any human probability, true miracles of the fountain of youth, and who, one day, all of a sudden, are transformed? "No, no, I'm only feeling a bit weary, a little bit low" Grandmother must have said. And the old doctor, who had known her for such a long time, must have hesitated while looking for the right words: "My dear lady, maybe you have tired yourself out". A pale smile: "Before, doctor, I used to do so many things. But now, it's all different; I don't do anything anymore". At the end, soberly, with dignity and a hint of humour, she may have said: "At my age, just imagine, it's absurd, I know, but I have had a serious loss, a chagrin d'amour". He would not have known what to say, there was nothing to be said. And his patient was so thin, so pale. The doctor had got her back on her feet, as best as he could, with medicines suitable for an elderly lady. "Things are better now" the doctor said at every appointment. In a certain sense that was also true. It was a question of growing old gracefully. Noone and nothing is eternal. Love least of all.

Grandmother said:

"Shall I pour you some of this whisky, then?"

Snatched from her thoughts, the girl nodded:

"Certainly".

"Do you want some ice? It's in the kitchen".

"No, I'll take it straight".

"Like me".

"Like you".

They drank to each other's health. Just the two of them. To tell the truth they had not drunk together in many years. Grandmother, after all, belonged to the era of vermouth or at most the era of dry martinis, hors d'oeuvres, silver trays covered with embroidered linen and, if anything was missing, the cook appeared, prompt and discreet. Or Enzo was there. One way or another one always came back to the same point: to Enzo. The girl thought of telling Grandmother that the reason she had come so rarely during those years was that Enzo was not there and she had not wanted to find the empty space. The two of them did not have anything to say to each other; there was nothing to say and it would have been a mistake to speak. So she used to meet Grandmother in the courtyard. Or she often came there with Mother.

In the autumn, after the summer when she had begun to smoke regularly, the girl had threatened to drop out of high school. She had even gone to live with some school companions two or three times. When the fury against her mother had reached its peak, she had found Grandmother again, but a different Grandmother. One day she had run into the courtyard, without an umbrella, under the October rain; she had stopped suddenly upon seeing her. Grandmother stood there, alone in the building entrance like a parcel from the post office. She had not even understood why she was there, what compelled Grandmother to wait there. She had her usual elegant appearance, impeccable in her suit, shoes and bag. Her usual style and even her fine figure had returned; the girl vaguely remembered that her mother had told her that the doctor had hit on the right cure. But her eyes betrayed her; they no longer had that look of flickering flame. She looked into the void.

"Grandmother!" She had stopped dead right in front of her, water dripping down the collar of her jacket.

"Darling!" Something flowed into her face and eyes again, but it gave her, however, an immediate feeling of sorrow.

"Darling" she repeated with pain, but also with the absolute will not to start suffering again.

At that moment Mother had arrived.

"Ah!" she had noted. "You are here too!" Then she had continued in her bossy way: "Let's go, let's not stand here, it's awfully damp. Grandmother will catch cold".

That nurse's tone was typical of her mother, at the time, but the girl also blamed her Grandmother because she let herself be manipulated. The old lady was a pawn in her daughter's hands. Rather than betraying her granddaughter, she was betraying herself.

"Goodbye then" the girl had cut the meeting short and started to go. Behind her she had heard an affectionate voice.

"Goodbye, darling. Goodbye, love".

Later on her mother had not missed the opportunity to admonish her:

"You might look after Grandmother a bit more".

But she had not answered, because she did not accept advice on the subject of Grandmother.

"What about Luigi?"

The question brought the girl once more back to the present. She would have liked to explain to her that at that moment Luigi was important because he was the reason they were together today. For the first time after so many years they were talking to each other again, not limiting themselves to the frivolous and optimistic summary of the girl's life. She had got into the habit of telling her: things are ok, and then little by little, in the middle of the full colour pamphlets of trips around the world, to Greece, Macedonia, Spain, Turkey, she would rattle off some of her private difficulties. No, she had no boyfriends, nobody special; no, she wanted to study something else at University; yes, those friends were nice, but no good for another trip together. She offered a toned down sweetened version of events, the kind offered to elderly people, to spare them suffering and worry and especially to prevent them from inquiring further. But with Grandmother these tactics did not work very well. Grandmother stopped asking straightaway, as if it were not worth while.

"So, what about Luigi?"

"Things are ok".

Grandmother shook her head with deep disappointment.

"You are always the same. Just as when you were little and had to announce the worst disasters: it's all right, you began by saying. How can you say things are all right with Luigi? Ten minutes ago you were crying! Come on, who are you kidding?"

The girl would have liked to sob even now.

The darkness was falling, a cold January evening. There was no longer the cook there to close the shutters. It felt cold just to look at the windows with the old curtains. This evening she was there to close the shutters. But what about the other evenings, when Grandmother was alone, immobile in her armchair, staring at the dark that was closing on her?

"I want the child, do you understand? But I don't want to leave here, you see? You keep asking funny questions: what's Luigi like, are we going to get married or not".

"Don't shout" said Grandmother sweetly. "Everybody can hear you".

"I have known Luigi ever since the sit-in at the University. Do you remember the sit-in?"[1]

"Yes indeed" said Grandmother. "Indeed I remember it. That famous evening".

It was certainly a famous evening. Between February and March, when it was almost spring, but it was cold, and it had happened before Enzo's abandonment.

Grandmother came out, as she never did. Mother and Giovanni were both frightened stiff that she might go to protest at the high school that evening: she and her friends took turns. Ever since she was born, her mother had been waiting for some tragedy, for the blow of destiny.

Even before dinner Grandmother had come over hatless and with her coat thrown over her shoulders, a sure sign of Mother's hurry and anxiety. Clearly Mother had asked her to stop the girl. She, the girl, was obsessed by the idea that others would go to the protest while she couldn't, that Sergio would be there and she would miss the chance of seeing him again. The occupation also meant that she could sleep with her boyfriend during night hours.

Against all expectations, Grandmother had said:

"Let her go. Let her live like other young people, for once, let her be like all the others. She cannot live forever divided between Italy and America, between your dominating presence and an absent father".

A great silence had followed. Her mother said: "Go, then, if Grandmother allows it. Even in this household, she is the boss".

She saw the girl hesitate, in fact she was waiting, she did not feel like doing anything anymore.

"Get out" she screamed.

"Go, darling" Grandmother said more softly, but her eyes were hard. Even Grandmother held her responsible for the scene.

That evening she met Luigi. It was raining when she arrived at the school. The desks had been moved and piled up, and in the middle there were the sleeping bags and cots. There was the usual smell of chalk and of an airless space, but also the sensation of sleeping together in group, as in a mountain hut.

In the classroom were gathered people from different grades and even from different schools. Some were university students. She had very few friends, only acquaintances. And everyone knew that this would be the last evening of the protest.

She had gone to the auditorium for the assembly: a university student was speaking. He had a big head of thick, brown hair and a pleasant face. But she did not feel like listening to anyone that evening. When she went back to the classroom, she discovered that they were all more or less in couples, in sleeping bags or under the blankets. She couldn't fall asleep on the cot somebody had loaned her.

While she was there with her eyes shut and the noise of the rain that could not calm her down, somebody lay down next to her, on the blanket.

"May I?" he had asked.

It was the university student from the assembly. He began to talk to her in a soft voice. He said he had come to that school because they had sent him there, but he did not believe very much in sit-ins, especially at high schools. He said very little about himself. And suddenly he asked her:

"Have you been crying?"

She had nodded.

"Pull yourself together".

He spoke kindly. His voice helped her fall asleep. When she awoke, he had gone away. Anyhow, it was morning.

"So" said Grandmother, "you have known Luigi for a long time, have you?"

"Well, yes. But I met him again only recently".

"Grandmother got up again, made her way towards the cabinet, shut the doors of the bar and turned to her.

"Listen to me" she said in a loud voice. "I am going to take care of Mother. She won't make a fuss. On the contrary" she smiled maliciously, "she will be very happy. At any rate, don't worry, think about yourself and your health" she hesitated again, "and your child. Since you are expecting one. The only thing that you must do is arrange a visit with the famous Luigi for me. And let me know in advance, because I want to go to the hairdresser before meeting him."

CHAPTER 5

The girl never had the chance to explain Grandmother how things had really gone. During the whole month of November, after meeting the girl in black, she had felt freed from worries. After her period came that month, she felt a pleasant weariness. She wondered whether it would be her last one or next to last one, and she enjoyed it like a beach she was about to abandon.

She met Luigi at the end of November. One afternoon, towards evening, while she was looking at the new books on the front counter of a downtown book store, she felt somebody touch her shoulder. In front of her, she saw the face of so many years before, but she remembered him as being taller. Of course, he had also put on weight. In his hair, which he wore fairly long and a little bit tousled, there were some grey threads and his expression, however pleasant, had grown sad".

"Would you like to go out?" suggested Luigi.

He decisively declined to drive the girl's car, sitting next to her as if he wanted to be driven. Almost immediately, however, he started giving directions.

"Surely you're not going through the city. Take this route. No, take that other street, we will come out exactly on the main street. Is it one way? No matter. Turn to the right, hurry, the traffic cop didn't see you".

In the meantime evening had fallen on Piazza del Popolo, on the churches, on the obelisk. The girl felt her life become lighter.

"Shall we take the Lungotevere?"

"Why not?"

Luigi's arm held the girl's seat, as if to guide her. His hand, which had been resting on the collar of her old wolf jacket, had slid under the collar to caress her.

"Well done Luigi! Not bad at all, Luigi," thought the girl. His fingers, in fact, moved slowly but intensely on the nape of her neck. It amused her to feel them. In the meantime she observed Luigi's profile, next to her, so still and impenetrable.

Along the almost empty Lungotevere the car ran smoothly. Luigi's fingers became more urgent.

"What do you say about a left turn here? If you don't mind, that is."

She played the game:

"All right, left turn".

After a few blocks he removed his hand and straightened himself up:

"We're here".

Outside the car, under the chilly darkness of the sky, the girl felt as if she were in a new place, one she had never seen. It was the Lungotevere, not too far from her home, but the clear night and the air's rarefaction expanded it, rendering it unrecognizable, almost bewitched.

"Here we are", said Luigi, under one of the apartment buildings, not far from the bridge.

The very tall and massive entrance door opened onto a passage, which with its friezes, stuccos and columns, had the dignity of a ballroom. At the end was a flight of stairs, nooks and crannies. The elevator left them on a wide landing, which dominated the intersecting perspectives of the flights of stairs making them appear to meet and then diverge and separate. A brass plate displayed Luigi's name.

The girl marvelled:

"Have we arrived?"

"Oh, for God's sake" Luigi dismissed his family with a gloomy wave of his arm. "It's further up. But let's be quiet. They are terrible".

As a matter of fact they climbed only a few steps. And it was certainly not an attic, but rather a magnificent roof-terrace above Rome, above the river and the monuments and the baroque churches on the other side, bathed in the moonlight.

"This is a world upside down. This is not Rome."

He stood next to her, in front of the large window which framed the wide sky and the night.

"And if it were not Rome, what might it be?"

"This white, enchanted light could be St. Petersburg, or Vienna, or Santo Stefano."

"You mean a place faraway from everything. A place to visit."

He knew how to play the game. He was determined and insistent, but enjoyed seeing where her fantasy would take her. He kept watching her, giving the impression that he did not want to let her go. This was a novelty. For a long time she had felt that nobody was interested in her and that her friends, her contemporaries, men and women, had only problems and complicated lives.

Luigi pulled aside the curtains, switched on the lamps and also lit the fire in a large fireplace, afraid that she might be cold. The girl felt her desire for him, while he was busy with his logs, on his knees, curved with his back to her. Between his sweater and the belt of his trousers, he revealed a strip of naked back which had a groove in the middle that widened down to his hips. The girl followed it from the point where it began to where, dark and forbidden, it lost itself inside the trousers.

In bed, she found him insistent, voracious. He had an almost animal like mouth, which he used to arouse her. He was certainly skilful, more mature that anyone else she had met so far. And he had an obstinate will to make her alive and to penetrate her.

When she went downstairs alone, in the icy night, she recalled his insistence as a promise she had made to herself.

CHAPTER 6

December, immediately afterwards, announced itself with clear, light blue skies, swept by the north wind. Miraculously it remained this way until Christmas. The girl felt that in that crystal-like clarity there was something special, that had to be seized at all costs. She thought about her project. It was a project of beginning and of accomplishment. The accomplishment foresaw a birth and, for the moment, this involvement in her project remained hers alone.

She placed that dazzling December within an ancient and ever repeating sequence of events. The girl had the impression she was in a clear and sunny glade, beaten by the wind, in the same way so many lonely women, before her, had found themselves concentrating on the expectation, on the event to come.

As for Luigi, she saw him only in the evenings and it wasn't even clear where he had been. He was a creature of shadow and mystery and belonged to the nocturnal part of those days. In the shadows, Luigi also loved to leave the places where he worked and the people he frequented behind him. He liked to show up suddenly only to go back to towns at which he hinted obscurely, without ever specifying names or jobs. Those places might be very near or be located further, be just outside Rome or at one or two hours' distance in Umbria or Tuscany. But, in Luigi's words, they all possessed the same character of necessity, of coercion, almost of slavery, with which he loved to surround his family too. On the whole, in Luigi's practical life there was an aura of necessity, or rather of fatality. He spoke of the places and the people to whom he devoted himself as if they were a destiny which had befallen him and from which he could not escape.

As a result, their meetings were short, occasional and also sudden. They were all grounded in the present: the girl's car or Luigi's attic. However, from time to time, these places acquired the role of a magic circle which enclosed them, thanks to his words. The girl, all taken by her idea, accepted this precarious relationship, which anyhow was consistent with the character of the year that was nearly over. She did not want to penetrate the mystery of Luigi, but she liked the fact that this mystery, so unrelated to her, should become intimate during their encounters. She liked the fact that Luigi's rigid, almost priestly nature, would bend to stamp on her a seal, a mark and would become tender and human in the effort of conquering her.

It seemed to her, moreover, that those rapid and unplanned encounters were not arbitrary at all and that for Luigi they were not as unforeseen as he wanted her to believe. In fact, when he emerged from his shadows, Luigi looked hard to create a dialogue with the girl's life and thoughts. He enquired obstinately about what she had done, how she had spent the hours far away from him. He shared with her the boredom of her daily routine.

"School, translations. How boring" he said. "You must write. You must express yourself. It's the only thing that counts. Forget everything else".

Inwardly the girl agreed with him and would have gladly left behind what Luigi called the rest, that is, her daily routines. But for her to be happy, at the moment the only important thing was her accomplishment, the future birth, even if she sensed that this would involve the end, not only of her relationship with Luigi and of their present encounters, but of all the world she had known until now. The fact was that she wished for something extra, a kind of present, and she wanted it now, and life must give it to her now, at that precise moment, because she was young, because she was ready to receive it and did not want to wait. She would have liked to explain to Luigi that this too meant expressing oneself; in fact it was creative and perhaps even more. It meant a knowledge that she did not want to postpone: the exploration of an event which she was entitled to, as a woman, but which could also pass next to her without touching her and which she could in no way give up.

The shadows were suited for Luigi, who kept alternatively withdrawing and leaning forward: she, instead, needed the glade, the clarity, the waiting. In this way, inevitably, there was a misunderstanding between them and, even while speaking of the same things, even while making love to each other, they pursued different aims. Their roads which, according to Luigi, should have run in parallel lines, in reality diverged. On the one hand Luigi, with a force and obstinacy that contrasted with his frequent and sudden disappearances, wanted to imprint on the girl the sign of his form and of his possession. She, on the other hand, was easily distracted and caught in the circular motion of her obsession. Two different, almost opposite paths, which, however, seemed to join in their encounters, in their embraces.

After a few days of silence, Luigi appeared at midday, an unusual hour for him, and suggested a trip. He had, he said, a half day off, even if it was not clear from what. The girl marvelled:

"But you don't like going away, isn't that true?"

He shrugged his shoulders:

"You like it".

The Sabine mountains had purple, wintery, shadows; the cypresses were almost black, while a golden phosphorescence in the afternoon sun, suggested brevity and closure. The meaning of the trip was only in the flight of the hours, which would soon plunge into the long winter night. In the alleyways already engulfed in shadow, the perfume of bread mingled with light mists.

They differed just in what seemed to the girl to be the simplest interpretation, the only evident one.

"What about poverty?" asked Luigi. "These miserable lives?"

"Why miserable? It is a beautiful, serene village. Look at these ancient houses".

"You don't know what there is inside. You have no idea".

It was clear that their quarrel went beyond the occasion, beyond that winter afternoon with its fiery sunset on the great plain of Rome.

Luigi claimed the supremacy of another world, tragic, isolated, separated. For the girl, on that day, only the visible, the future and birth counted.

In the silence of the car Luigi's voice sounded, by contrast, tender almost compassionate.

"I have to go away. For a few days. Another village like this one".

"So?"

"Nothing. We are not going to see each other for a while".

At the moment, when she realized that Luigi's projects diverged from hers and took him away towards an unknown that would make him unreachable, the girl felt her hope waning. For some reason that was not clear even to her, by the end of December her option would expire, and with the option, her project would also disappear.

"Then, it's over".

"What do you mean?"

The mechanism of vengeance escaped Luigi, who was ready at most for sadness.

"I'll return, later on".

"It doesn't matter any more. The discussion is closed, Luigi".

"But why?"

Now he was the one who was coming out of the wood, faithful to his oscillating movement, which made him hide and show himself in turn. He was suggesting the encounter in the glade, bringing her close to her goal, unaware of the betrayal plotted by the girl at his expenses, unaware of the girl's desire, a desire that could not ever be exchanged with company, solidarity or friendship.

"Don't act like that. Not like that. Come up with me in the attic. Then we'll see".

In bed, in front of the large window which, this time, framed a cloudy, almost obscure sky, Luigi's head lay on her breast, his face hidden. In her mind the girl implored him:

"One more time, make love to me Luigi, make love to me as much as you can".

Luigi whispered in her ear:

"I love you".

Then the girl abandoned herself:

"At last. Stay inside me. Everything will be alright, Luigi".

CHAPTER 7

Rome is always portentous towards Christmas time. Spring seems just round the corner but doesn't arrive, in fact it moves further and further away because of the purity of the lights, and the intricate severity which the reflexions of the bare branches embroider on the *façades* at midday.

That year the girl felt the opposite order of things intersecting within herself as well. Everything was radiant, but she remained unaware of it. After her encounter with Luigi, that short period of December resembled death rather than birth, and life and death mingled within her, since she was afraid of that beginning to which she had abandoned herself.

She was very eager for the days to pass taking her to the fatal deadline: crossing that gap of fifteen-eighteen days that would reveal whether she was pregnant or not. This would decide her destiny: whether everything was settled for better or for worse, or whether everything had to start again. She did not want to try to find out before then. On the contrary, she was afraid of the moment she would learn the truth. As always, she abandoned herself to nature, though she was afraid of it, and to time, even though she kept wondering what it would bring with it.

Maybe in her case nothing had happened and she would never blossom like a waiting mimosa, with its rigid branches, always the same.

After postponing his departure for a few days, Luigi, who had not mentioned leaving again, suddenly let her know that he was taking the train the next morning. For the first time he also told her where he was going: Arezzo.

"I'll be back soon, you'll see".

"Of course".

The girl felt herself blushing inside for what, within herself, without really admitting it, she called deception, a treason perpetrated against the persons who trusted her. A treason which, against all moral laws, already bore its fruit, creating in her a tender yielding to life.

Instead Luigi was several days late, but his delay barely surprised her, busy as she was at listening to herself. By now she had entered an area of book-keeping, of double entry, in which dates, numbers and simple notions of gynaecology were linked together with a perverse and temporary whirling motion which left her drained. Her inner reality was always present, while concrete reality got out of focus: her work as a translator, her teaching duties, the students whose lives she barely knew, the friends whom she no longer contacted, because she did not know what to tell them until she was sure of her destiny. Even her family. Even Grandmother.

"We'll have to decide about Christmas dinner" her mother said one day, and the girl then realized that in a short time she would have to fight on two fronts: her own, intimate, anxious, already full of regrets or remorse, and the other, made of family ceremonies, of the ritual tribute to the holiday season.

On Thursday nothing happened and she moved the deadline to the evening. She tried to free her mind from every thought, but her brain registered in an implacable way the slightest stomach ache, even if barely stronger than the ripple of a veil of water.

Without even realizing it, at the first remote signal, she was already telling herself: "I'm going to be on. It's all over. It's coming" and the sun grew dark and December cold became sharp. Then the cramp, a small wave in the dark lake of her uterus, would die away, ebbing far from where it had come or from where perhaps it had never left, and the sun would shine again.

She went on like this for hours, with this sensitivity, by now a habitual companion in the folds of her brain, always on the look-out for pain. When she happened to stop, during the intervals between her trips from one part of the city to the next, she felt her thoughts throbbing inside her. And yet that subterranean world of hers, similar to a river or to a sea, also functioned as a compass: a subliminal indication of the hour, the day, the waiting periods, the probabilities, the approach to a yet unknown destination, but which turned out in any case to be made of pain and labour.

By Friday, she had not had her period, demonstrating two equally valid truths: that it would not come at all, or, that, on the contrary, as it had happened other times, it would arrive at the last possible moment, beyond all hope. As it had happened many other times. Which times? Many times. The last six or seven years were crowded with months, examples, circumstances, fears, that now got confused in her head, though they were clearly impressed against different individual backgrounds: offices, schools, sea, mountains, cars, camping trips, all characterized by a sudden merciful relief, like a divine absolution. If the end results were clear, much less clear were the men and reasons connected with the delays. In fact reasons and men, just as it had happened during the night with Luigi, had been replaced by a perverse and jet fearful trembling taste for risks.

The girl came back with painful pleasure to those days that by now had gone forever: it was a Friday, no, it was a Saturday; she had taken the train and was desperate, and then there was the arrival and the freedom; she had taken the pill and had made a mistake, no, in fact she had not taken it for a month and it was summer. And she felt suffocated in the net of victories which no longer counted, of *dénouements* which the following month had already erased. Suffocated by her persistent desire to destroy her calm, by creating a child or by avoiding creation at the last moment.

And in that small feminine arithmetic there was something excruciating and at the same time voluptuous, which no education, no progress, nor medical discovery would ever modify, to which no pill, calendar, diaphragm, spiral or cream would ever bring rationality. Between her planning and her vital flow there was inserted her need for adventure, that personal madness of hers which now, however, like so many other times before, she was ready to forsake.

In the evening, exhausted by the whirl of dates and calculations, tired of going back to a past that had not taught her anything, she stopped thinking for a while. The cramps, anyhow, appeared to her to be skin-deep, ready to come out, arrogant and judgmental.

"What did you do today?" It was Luigi, on the phone. "In any case, tomorrow I'm coming back".

"Tomorrow?" Her voice broke in her throat.

The next day her fate would be decided, if not objectively, at least within her. The next day she would understand whether this time was different from all the others, whether the final goal would be reached, or whether her fate would remain still hidden. The next day she woke up, determined not to suffer any longer. Her hidden interlocutor seemed indifferent, like her, or at least asleep. The girl did not despair even when, at midday, she felt pains, deep stirs, of an ancient, telluric and implacable nature. By now even her capacity to despair had run out.

Towards evening, instead, she acquired absolute certainty. No period would come now. The landscape had changed, by now she was somewhere else. After all the moons which had made fun of her up to the last, this December moon was not mocking her.

Slowly, on foot, she crossed a bridge on the Tiber: it was dusk, the end of a sweet and very beautiful day, which still lingered in the phosphorescence of the air, in the mist which was now lit by the last light. The barges, orange, multicoloured wooden structures on the river's surface, were reflected in the slow water, painting a fantastic, upside down world. Her world too was upside down, with unknown rules and roads, a world she had desired desperately for such a long time, and which now, however, she feared, because she could not share it with anyone

Once he had come back, Luigi asked with his usual didactic obstinacy:

"Did you work? Did you finally decide to write? What did you do?"

"Nothing".

She would have liked to explain to Luigi that she could not speak, that, perhaps, with her decision, with her pregnancy, she had erased for herself the existence of the attic, the sight of the Roman St. Petersburg, everything they had looked at together. She would have liked to explain that this was a creation, which, for the moment, put everything aside.

Anyhow Luigi's irritation grew, in fact rose like a tide with the passing of days, with the intensification of the festive preparations, the pealing of bells, the honking of horns and the traffic jams. The very act of talking to him became practically impossible.

He spoke by fits and starts and mangled his sentences:

"See each other? Tomorrow? For heaven's sake. There is the family. The whole family. Lots of them. And then, what does it matter? It's all so foolish. Let's postpone our meeting to later on, later on".

Luigi's days threatened to become indefinite but implacable deadlines and rituals: meals, panettoni, mistletoe, wishes, presents.

Instead, for the girl, the light, the hours, the flavours of the season were similar to all the other years. Also similar was the pale smile of Grandmother, who now only two or three times a year bestowed the favour of her presence on Mother's artificial conviviality and Giovanni's obtuse affability. When she was with the three of them, who were so unchanged and unaware, the girl felt her condition of imminent exile and emargination becoming really heartbreaking.

"What's the matter, are you a bit tired?"

During Christmas dinner Grandmother had looked at her two or three times and had seemed lost in thought. Now, warned by her silence that was even more obstinate than usual, she seemed anxious to release her at least from her family obligations.

"Soon I shall have a little rest. Don't stand on ceremony, darling, if you have to leave early".

The girl would have really liked to disappear, but she did not know where. In front of her there stood a very long evening which was just starting to brush against the sky, and the hostile city concealed a

Luigi, lost in heaven knows what recesses of houses and kinships.

She said:

"Yes, maybe". And after a brief pause:

"All right, I'll go then".

She got up with a movement that immediately left her tired, like a woman who is several months pregnant. Even her mother noticed it:

"Is something bothering you?"

Grandmother, who was more perceptive, thought it over and contradicting herself said:

"But it's so cold outside. Do you really have to go out?"

Yes, thought the girl, because it was equally impossible for her to speak or to remain sitting in silence next to her Grandmother. It really was necessary for her to go out. To go out, carrying a burden that was not yet physical, but seemed so to her already, and for this reason she had to share it and unload it. A burden that was a joy, a present that no one had given her and yet had to be forgiven, because it was also a pain, and she did not have the courage to keep it to herself. Therefore she was going to confess it, though she regretted even now of having to leave her condition of anonymity which she could not bear any longer.

"No, no, I'm going out".

In the darkness of the car, the rear-view mirror seemed to send back to her not the road, but the family group, Grandmother, Mother, Giovanni. The ancient cohesion, the barrier, the shoal that had been there for so many years, was already far behind her, separated from her by news that would have a distorting effect even on them.

"Oh, it's you".

Behind Luigi's voice, on the phone, there was no background noise. As usual, she couldn't understand from which family, from which festivities he emerged.

"Disturb me? Not at all. Yes, yes, dinner is over, quite over. All right, I'm coming". He hesitated for a second. "If you really want to. But have you got the car? All right, then, at the coffee bar down below".

In the Lungotevere coffee bar, a large locale with columns, worn by time but of ancient nobility, there could be found a very modern and shining espresso machine, tall pastry store counters decorated in white and gold, pretty Vienna chairs and chairs from the thirties with a veneer of shining wood. The coffee bar had long been emptied by the frantic search for panettoni, but a trace of the hectic activities remained in the pale face of the cashier, the barmen and the two ladies at the counter. In low voices they talked to each other, isolated like the girl, in the middle of the gregarious, festive city. Within two hours, at most, their loneliness would be over and, detached finally from the work, immersed in the family rituals that were waiting for them, they would be kissed, like everyone, by the Christmas blessing.

In the almost total darkness of the second room, hidden between the columns, two or three couples of uncertain age, looking like employees, murmured in even lower voices, with their mouths close to each other in order to communicate, to eat, or simply to demonstrate that they were alive; clandestine deserters, condemned to a Christmas made of loneliness and of faint lights.

Luigi's face, hesitating at the room's entrance, gave the measure of the scene's squalor. Only at the last minute did he discover the girl sitting in the remotest corner. He stared at her almost incredulous.

"Ah, is that you?"

"I had to see you".

"Now?"

The sentence could mean anything, an allusion at the just finished Christmas dinner, or to the season, or, worse, to his frame of mind, which had once more become inscrutable and full of danger. In the meantime, he sat down in a tired way, unbuttoned his coat, and passed his hand through his hair which was wet with dampness. None of his gestures, though, appeared friendly or familiar, and the girl couldn't help looking at all those gestures as if she had been seized by a kind of terrifying panic.

However he was the one who made an effort to get back to normal, to bring her back to reality, to make the last attempt to recreate their intimacy, which was so irreparably far away.

"Darling. What happened?"

"I'll tell you".

"Now, here?"

She should have, might have kept quiet, if a kind of morbid curiosity had not driven her to observe, as if it concerned another person, the disaster that was about to happen: the extraordinary invention that she had set up and that now reached its epilogue. The mirrors, the Christmas decoration, the mistletoe, the holly; and in the other room, the scene lit by the intermittent lights of the sinister little tree, placed next to the cash register. A miracle of monstrosity, the exact opposite of the theatre for children, where all the characters should appear lovely, united in a brief happiness. Now a great silence had congealed on the marble tables and over the graceful Vienna chairs: it seemed as if the other couples, with their heads drawn close, were observing them with concern.

"Well, tell me" Luigi urged her.

The girl looked at herself in the large gilded mirror from Paris: she saw she was young, perhaps also beautiful, with her dark eyes that flashed, and the raised fur collar that framed her hair. At least half-length, down to the waist she was still mobile, free to go out, travel and leave that sad coffee bar behind her. But it was only an instant and then the image became opaque once more. She would never be alone and mobile again, even if she gave up her dream to fulfill the prophecy of the girl in black. She lowered her eyes, looking inside her open jacket, as if she could see already a bulge. The image had been betrayed and now was destined to disappear. Or rather, after so many years and uncertainties, the image had betrayed itself out of tiredness.

"And so?"

There was, perhaps, some strategy she could use, but the girl immediately gave it up. She had never been good with strategies, she even lost when she played checkers with Cesira. It is useless to plan the first move, when you will certainly lose the last one, or the one before, or yet another one. To have won the match between herself and her womb, thought the girl, had already been very skilful. For the match with Luigi, she would need the conviction that she was right.

"They are closing" Luigi announced with relief.

It was true; the waiters were staring at the clients, ready to resort even to cruelty in order to send them away. Their long vigil was coming to an end, thought the girl. And hers would now begin.

"The bill" Luigi asked the old arthritic waiter imperiously.

They left with a heavy step, and immediately a clanking noise resounded at their back: the coffee bar's shutters were being lowered with force. All of a sudden the sign was turned off.

They were alone in the street. Above their heads was a starry sky, perfect for Christmas.

"How are you going to get home?"

"I have the car, I told you" said the girl softly.

"What did you want to speak to me about?" insisted Luigi, going decisively in the direction of the river.

There was no noise in the night. Only a few cars glided silently on the bridge and disappeared, lost into the night. The girl felt she had no room left. In front of her, the river with its cold breath; at her back, the closed coffee bar and her car round the corner, too far away to be reached for the moment. Luigi, who was smoking close by, did not look either at her, or at the river, or at the sky. He too was rooted to the asphalt, already crushed by the weight that was about to crumble on him. She closed her eyes, then, opening them again, she saw confused, unfamiliar lights on the other bank. "Luigi" she said. "I wanted a baby. I am expecting".

Nobody passed by, there was no noise.

"My God" said Luigi, "what a mess we have made".

CHAPTER 8

Prisca's birth took place some seven months later. The girl spent that crucial date, or rather the day before, in another coffee bar. It was the Casina Valadier, on the Pincio, at the end of July; she was with Grandmother.

Since she happened to be in Grandmother's house that morning, she said on a whim:

"I'm so happy to be here with you. Now I'm really on holidays. We'll do so many things together, Rome is still so pleasant, it's not hot at all. I feel really well. Quite fine. You don't want to go away on holidays immediately, as mother says, do you? Won't you wait a few days to know what I shall do?"

"One thing at a time, let's not make plans" said Grandmother. "We'll see. First of all you must go to the doctor for that darned examination you have postponed so many times. Get the obstetrician to explain everything to you. And don't overtire yourself".

Grandmother wanted to say more or less what her mother was constantly repeating to her. The latter was always worried about everything, and sometimes stared at her in silence with a gloomy air and a furrow that formed itself in the middle of her brow. Or she came up with stories of very difficult births. Grandmother, instead, limited herself to giving her a few practical suggestions and reassuring her not to worry. During all those months, Grandmother had remained the same as always, seemingly detached but attentive. She had met Luigi and thought him nice, but after the meeting she never returned to the subject of marriage, never again asked about plans for the future, after the birth of the baby. The girl had never understood how she had managed to placate Mother's reactions and create a climate of silence if not of serenity around the pregnancy.

That winter and spring she had had so little time for herself, so the girl felt, on that day, a great desire to do something. When she heard that Grandmother had made an appointment with an old cousin of hers that afternoon, she decided to go along with her:

"I am going with you. The Pincio must be very beautiful at sunset. Don't tell me you don't want me".

"What nonsense, darling. Of course I want you to come. But you are already so huge and you look a bit tired. And then you know what Nené is like; she talks all the time about her stories, her trips. I don't think it would be much fun for you".

Instead it had been fun and worthwhile, as the girl had assumed in the morning. A very beautiful occasion because that afternoon represented a unique moment which framed many others. They were on the great terrace that overlooked Rome, full of festive people, in a summer mood between city and holiday. The other moments included first of all the periodic irruptions of Nené, back from long journeys and cruises from which she carried tangible signs such as brochures and photographs, and tales which all resembled each other, in spite of the different places. She remembered other, earlier sunsets, when she was a child at the coffee bar with Grandmother, or with Grandmother and Mother, or with Enzo and Grandmother, and always, on the table, there was a bowl of ice cream with the spoon immersed in a glass of water, and the sea breeze which rose to move the leaves, like a sudden warning of the passage of time.

In any case, while Grandmother and Nené chatted, she perceived the conversation like the instalment of a long novel which was now coming to the end, with the disappearance of many characters who had left for journeys from which they would not bring back echoes or for holidays of which they would not provide news. All of a sudden she saw them changed: two ladies who still distinguished themselves by the classical, refined, always fashionable discretion of their manner of dressing, but were exhausted by the effort of so many summers similar to this one and of winters even harsher than the past one. Ladies who had been rendered fragile by too many adaptations to temperatures difficult to bear, to sudden changes of season, tackled each time with courage and humour, hope and imagination.

Nené lightly touched and passed around timetables and shiny and enticing travel brochures, but this time, the girl noticed, the old fingers, though always manicured, moved without the greed they had before, as if Nené no longer enjoyed living life to the full. And Grandmother, always so courteous and active in supporting her, had hardly glanced at them.

They were now talking of trips which were closer and yet at the same time more distant: the Alps, the hills and the countryside where they had spent their youth, whose events and precise circumstances they seemed to want to find again and set within their context with a curious, almost incongruous obstinacy. Traces on the sand, thought the girl, intelligible only to Grandmother and Nené, traces which no one would care about once the two women were gone. Changing the subject unexpectedly, Nené observed:

"The town where Luigi lives must be very beautiful".

Then she stopped. She had perhaps been on the point of asking why the girl had not stopped in that town, had not lived her pregnancy near Luigi, but something in Grandmother's expression, a remainder of their old understanding as girls, had dissuaded her from going on.

"Luigi works a little far away from the town. In a Mental Health Institute".

"These are all new professions" asserted Nené. "I don't understand them at all".

"He works at rehabilitating misfits".

"That's interesting" said Nené. "He must be very busy. You were right not to go there, because towns are never much fun".

No, the girl had never stopped in Luigi's town. On the contrary, she had been afraid of it. In Rome her belly, her new condition, became part of everyday life. Few words, outwardly calm and in any case definitive, were enough to maintain the semblance of normality: "No, everything is fine. Yes, of course I'm still working. More or less the same life. No, I am not tired. Fortunately summer is coming. The baby should be born in September. Certainly, I shall soon take maternity leave. Then we shall see".

Change, evolution and even defeat were unavoidable, evident phases and the city assimilated them all. Her interlocutors, different among themselves, were colleagues, friends, casual acquaintances and they had other things to do besides putting together the various threads of her story. They were not even interested in the prologue: it might be Luigi or another one, here or elsewhere, what mattered was how the story would end, how difficulties would be faced.

"Why don't you take your maternity leave now? Take it easy, rest. Maybe you can go away". These were conventional sentences, curiosity stopped there.

In the smaller town, however, she immediately felt ill at ease whenever Luigi came to pick her up, as if in mourning, with sad affection. And their game of silences and allusions continued during her brief stays and the meals they had in the little house, at the end of a lane. It was an old house, badly renovated, with second rate materials, icy cold tiles which had replaced the ancient brick floor, small rooms made from ample and noble spaces which had been divided up. With its bare look, the house corresponded too much to the new Luigi, who sometimes closed himself off in a gloomy silence. But it did not last long, just as the girl's visit lasted very little. Only twice, in all those months, did they return to being their old selves. There was one day in spring when looking out of a window which opened onto the valley, the girl finally saw the big mountain rise out of the haze. Suddenly in its sinuous and undulating shape the body of a woman emerged. Lying down, or rather face downwards, with the hollow at the back that climbed up gently, to descend into the thigh, the calf, the ankle, the body seemed to cut across the window disappearing into the hills and into nothing.

Luigi surprised her while with a pen in her hand she was staring at the shape.

"Try and fix her on paper just as you see her".

He is right, thought the girl without hostility, Luigi is right and has understood that this woman lying face down is beautiful and that I like her.

There was also another evening. It was almost summer and they happened to be near a lake. Surrounded by green, the lake was small, with reeds and calm waters. Some people were fishing in silence. On the banks there was a coffee bar, which was also very small, where they sold only ham sandwiches, chewing gum, candies and fruit juices. Behind the counter there stood out a foreign lady, no longer young, tall and beautiful, with an oddly fashionable appearance. She and Luigi knew each other and they talked to each other quietly. That evening the girl felt in peace.

In a loud voice, turning to Grandmother and Nené, she informed them:

"Near the town, there are mountains, lakes. Very beautiful places".

"I can imagine" answered Nené. "I would love to see them".

"Let's go" said Grandmother. "It's late". And, turning to Nené, she added: "She must not get too tired. Tomorrow she must go to the obstetrician".

It was really late and the party, that little party, was over. The terrace overlooking Rome was slowly emptying; everyone was leaving to continue the evening somewhere else: at the seaside, at the Castelli. Even Grandmother and Nené banished her away from it to her destiny of waiting, medical examinations and rest.

"Have you decided where you are going to go this summer? You have my address: please don't leave me without news".

Nené could not stand to live without some tie to the future: places, dates, another appointment. Once more it was Grandmother who acted as intermediary playing for time:

"No, nothing has been decided yet. But we shall do something. And anyway let's keep in touch".

"Next time I bet we shall come here with the baby" asserted Nené, starting towards the exit, arm in arm with Grandmother whom she delicately supported.

No, thought the girl, it's not true: this meeting remains unique and unrepeatable. Something is changing, has already changed.

The summer dusk was slipping away and in the light traffic of the end of the season, she drove home with a slightly intoxicated automatism. She was cheered up by the exceptional presence of Grandmother, sitting next to her. She caught sight of her profile under the raised brim of her white hat, and then the trim neckline of her beautiful silk dress in black and white, as was fashionable that year. It was a dress, however, that she thought she had seen for many summers.

"You were right to come" Grandmother said. "But are you feeling all right, now, aren't you tired?"

"Don't worry, everything is all right".

Yes, thought the girl, I am feeling very well. And she felt close to Grandmother - joined to her by this outing, by the Casina Valadier, by this brief escape - as she had not been for months. Grandmother was pried away from her apartment, from the blackmail of her unruly servants, and she from the obsession of her anomalous state. They were both free and close to each other.

"How beautiful the summer is. How a long it has been since I have not gone out like this" said Grandmother.

I would like to know, thought the girl. They were already in Via Veneto and in a short time they would turn down the street where she lived: there were so few people around. She could ask now. When would they be alone, together, again, in the car?

She would have liked to ask, after such a long time, how everything had gone. At which moment, if there had ever been one, had Grandmother realized that the show might end and that the main actor would withdraw cautiously, perhaps gently, but definitively, and disappear from the horizon?

The minutes slipped away, the unique occasion was about to disappear and she would never know. If only she had the courage to speak to Grandmother, to ask her: Enzo, a part of our life, yours and mine, where is he? Is he dead only for us or for everybody? Or alive only for you and me? Why don't you tell me, now that we are alone, and we remember the same things and have the same thoughts?

"Here we are at home" said Grandmother.

"You know" said the girl, "I'm feeling rather odd. I wouldn't be surprised if something were to happen".

"Keep calm, don't move, darling. I am going to tell Mother".

Then, with a quick mechanism, she and her heavy, awkward body were compelled to follow a set course, marked by consultations, hospital beds and more beds, examinations, decisions, words of which only senseless sounds reached her, which, however, in that world that to her was incomprehensible, might have some meaning.

On the side of these transit lanes there appeared one or two known faces. Luigi's face did not appear at all. But it was a triumph which she could not communicate to him and which only he would understand: his absence did not hurt her at all. Nothing really hurt her. Everything was opaque and deadened, like her labour pains. Thanks to the injec-

tion which had long been discussed in the intense
secret meetings that were held next to her, the pains
arrived muffled and weak like waves on a deserted
shore. On the contrary her thoughts remained alert,
even if wonderfully free from any responsibility,
open only to receiving the extraordinary event that,
she suspected, would remain unique, not to be
duplicated and therefore absolutely not to be
missed.

In the course of the various stages, she heard
screams from other women, whom she would have
liked to silence. It did not even occur to her that she
was like them, that she might reveal herself in the
same cowardly and coarse way, that she too might
somehow disturb the great moment. Her voice, however, when she answered questions, sounded broken
and hoarse even to her ears. She was annoyed by the
usual split that persecuted her: to be outwardly a person like everybody else, at the mercy of nature, pain
and reactions that could not be controlled, and
inwardly incredibly shrewd and cheerfully curious.

Later even this did not matter any longer: she
was in a room, no, a cubicle, when she realized that
the day was partly gone and the sun filtered in
through the lowered blinds a different way. Before
her a large white clock with enormous and incredibly slow dials seemed to move implacably towards a
definitive hour. Once more her mind concentrated
on the dials, awake and free; detached from her
body, which was partially covered, very far away,
with many people toiling over it. At one point, from
that side, the bustle became more intense, and while
she was staring at the dials that showed twenty two
minutes past two, she heard a noise, a cry. She put
the two facts together and, beyond hope, trusting in
the miracle, she asked:

"Is the baby born?"

"Yes" they said, "a girl, all is well".

It was the present, then, the only present in her life that without anybody's help she had given herself, and it had the perfection of an exam that had been passed or of a love that had been enjoyed.

CHAPTER 9

T wenty days later, it was a season of implacable skies, plastered with heat, of thin dust that filtered through everywhere. Heroic and impossible defences were attempted against that sun that beat down ferociously until almost evening on the half closed shutters.

Ever since that morning Prisca, born as a promise of a companion with the same rights and the same ideas, would withdraw into a kind of cave or river bed. She appeared to be very small and somewhat in pain, as if she were still in the incubator that had protected her for two weeks. She was alternatively pale and red according to the temperatures and the hours, according to whether she had to eat or sleep or had other secret necessities. In any case, she was lost in that crib that did not belong to her, but had been borrowed from one of mother's friends, who had a daughter who once had gone to school with the girl.

Nothing was really hers or fitted her. Very little had been planned, and anyhow it had all been imagined or bought for an undefined season, completely different from the present one; for a different house where she would not live with the girl's mother. Prisca had many things which did not match, in temporary drawers that were out of place, nothing that resembled a real layette.

Like Prisca, she had outfits that did not match, in fact, to be precise, she felt she had nothing to wear. When she woke up in the morning in her narrow sin-

gle bed, which had become, all of a sudden, a raft of
solitude and widowhood, she would smell on herself
an ancestral mixture of pungent humours, milk and
blood, of which perhaps she had always had a fore-
boding. These humours did not melt, did not weld
together. They made her, or so it seemed to her,
sticky, swollen and exhausted at the same time. They
were resistant to soap and water, because they were
the obstinate symbol of this enormous parenthesis
of non sickness from which she could not yet escape.

Anyhow, she was another person, this too neither foreseen nor foreseeable, who now occupied
only a corner of her room's mirror, hung behind
Prisca's crib. A mirror she knew too well, which in
crucial moments had sent her back so many different images, even more dramatic than the present
one, but never so out of focus. Her light July tan had
become ashen, her hair fell down dull around her
thin face, her eyes had widened and were without
light.

She thought that, after all, in spite of the fact that
she had given birth, she still resembled a pregnant
mare, more fit for a stable than for a city apartment,
which was forever in shadow and yet pierced by
fierce arrows of sunlit dust.

How quickly the festive expectation experienced
at the Casina Valadier had disappeared. Where had
the deep June skies gone, the clouds that came from
a faraway sea, beyond the mountain ridge, creating
sudden shadows and granting long evenings filled
with broom flowers and linden? And November,
that muffled November of the girl in black, to which
light and happy era had it ever belonged?

August, settling down suddenly after Prisca's
birth, denied that there had ever been other seasons
and other days. Instead it had invaded the house in

the shape of misfortune, heat, intolerance, a secret but real threat to Prisca's tender existence.

"How are you doing?" Her mother knocked cautiously, without conviction, in a way that barely respected formalities. "Ah, you are awake".

The girl was just able to detach herself from the mirror by a fraction of a second and now she kept her voice, which was already choking with anger, in check.

"She slept well. I breastfed her".

Adding to the unintentionally generous information she said:

"Now she is sleeping".

"Did you feel the heat? I couldn't sleep a wink".

"Here inside it's not bad".

"Today it's going to be terrible. It was on the radio".

It seemed that in Prisca's birth her mother saw a vengeance of destiny being carried out, a vengeance which had been expected with pleasure and had finally become manifest: the seven-month baby, the worries caused by the birth, her daughter all alone, unmarried, without a companion, without assistance, in the heat of that terrible August. In that destruction of everybody's moral fibre, mother had the radio and the television as her allies. Both broadcast only terrifying information, up to the minute war bulletins, hammered with growing menace every two, four, six hours. The only thing they did not say on the radio was what fate August reserved for them. The radio did not say what was the real meaning of this August, and whether there was any hope of coping with it as it spread everywhere. It was a scourge, a plague of Egypt, a natural calamity made worse by carelessness and by the failure to observe

one or two of the ten commandments. It surrounded
them and threatened to sweep them away. In fact it
threatened to sweep Prisca away who, unlike Moses
and others like him, would not be saved by the
waters of the Nile. No she wolf, no nanny, no holidays, no father.

But what about the others, the girl caught herself
wondering in solitary and obsessive monologues,
what type of August did the others have, how was
their August? It did not seem possible to her that
anyone else would have a situation that was so con-
fusing, that caused such piercing pains, that became
an acid test by which to live or die, or survive with
frightening and irreparable losses of decimated feelings and sunken hopes. Surely for no one else, as for
her, did August roam through the apartment as a
dark and suffocating ghost, ready to attack. Her
apartment was lonely, isolated or else joined to the
rest of the world only by silent streets, humiliated
porters, closed shutters now reduced to slits. For no
one else, as for her, had August now become identified
with a personal misfortune, with an unintelligible
destiny into which the girl felt she had to throw herself headlong.

"Today is the third" said Mother.

The third, she repeated, touching the microscopic finger of Prisca's pink hand with one of her
fingers. How light was Mother's hand on the baby,
the girl thought to herself, how natural and different. How closely related was her joy to her blind
fury; maybe it was only the other face of fear.

"What are you planning to do?"

She felt like answering: I don't plan. Or, I plan
too much. I have been planning all night long. All
night I have asked myself why, between one breast
feeding and another, even when I was half asleep. I

must have done kilometres of thought, but going in a circle, like a donkey at the grindstone.

"What about?"

"Let's not start again, please. We have discussed it enough. This heat, the baby. She is too small. With this temperature, children should not stay in the city".

Her answers were terribly banal, worthy daughters of her mother's observations. Millions of newborn babies just born everywhere, in India, in the centre of Africa, even in Basilicata or in Saronno, remained in the city. She herself, during her faraway years in America, had spent the summer in very hot suburbs. And finally not everybody, like her mother's friends, could lead a healthy life. She hated her answers as much as she hated her mother's observations. In fact she saw them all together, some in bold face, others in italics, like a kind of catechism to be ignored.

But for her, when she was a child, there had been no torrid seasons: they were all mild, temperate seasons. She would trustingly put her hand into Mother's hand and enter the shallow water of beaches that were very large, clear and clean, and which might be in America or in Italy. Her mother was young, and often alone. Her mother was also pretty. Sometimes she was deep in thought. Sometimes there appeared next to her young men, not at all like Giovanni. Now her mother asserted with arrogance:

"After all, children don't ask to be born. It is useless to have children, if one is not ready to make some sacrifice".

Why speak of sacrifice, why cancel the clear beaches, the fresh June mornings of their brief season of happiness? After all her mother had also been a girl or at least a young woman with a daughter, as happy as she was about Prisca. Why should they persist, now, in a vengeful discussion, spoken in low voices simply not to wake up Prisca?

"Excuse me, please, but now I have to breast feed the baby".

Now she managed by herself, but on the first day, when she had just come back home, with her hands, not knowing what to do, she had been guided by her mother's gestures.

"How strange. I would never have believed it. You never forget", Mother had said, with a curious smile. As if she too had felt stirred and troubled, at the sight of the woman's breast, of the dark nipple with a disproportionate ring around it, grabbed by the newborn baby with instinctive aggression. "One remembers", she had repeated, with her face cleared by the enchantment of the brief passages, from the cradle to the changing table, the diapers, the gauze, each essential for Prisca's life. Then she had lowered her eyes, frightened by her daughter's involuntary and admiring trust.

"For heaven's sake. I'll leave immediately. I'm sorry".

Her mother's words now hissed in resentment: as always, as before. After a few days the novelty had disappeared, killed by August and by the many questions the girl had not answered: "Are you going to visit Luigi? How are you going to manage? What would you have done if I had not been there? You do have a house, a roof over your head, don't you? Who takes care of you, shops for you and thinks about all you need?"

"All right, now you can manage by yourself. I am going shopping before the heat becomes unbearable".

When Mother was young, she did everything with pleasure and never reproached her about anything.

"Starting tomorrow the butcher will be going on holidays. I must stock up for at least two days. I really don't know what we will do afterwards. Of course you are aware that the pharmacy is closing for vacation. Its turn to be on holidays begins today".

In the desert one had to start looking for the nearest oasis.

"The fruit seller is also closing. They are all going to the seaside together. The daughter-in-law has a two-year old child".

"And the supermarkets?"

"They will close by the middle of August, when, I imagine, we will still be at the same point where we are now. You remember that the cleaning lady is leaving us in five days, don't you?"

"What about Grandmother?"

"Please, let's avoid any misunderstanding and not put Grandmother's problem into the same pot. I think we have enough problems as it is. You know very well that Grandmother is here because you are here. The day you make a decision, she too will find some accommodation, she too will leave.

The main problem had not been mentioned for several days, but had remained lying in ambush: should she spend her holidays with them, Mother and Giovanni, or find something by herself and go away with whomsoever she wanted.

If only it had not been summer, thought the girl after hearing the door slam. If it had not been hot. If August had suddenly finished and miraculously abandoned her rooms. If she had the time to think and reflect. If the city had not been a ship to be aban-

doned, women and children first of course. If Prisca
had not been at risk of getting sick: heat strokes,
gastroenteritis, the mysterious and fulminating dis-
eases of the newborn, which were the stakes, the
Lord's vengeance, the unexpected which was lying
in wait. If Prisca had not had such a soft little head, if
she had not been so microscopic.

When spring was well on and hydrangeas were
blossoming, Enzo had disappeared. Sergio had gone
into hiding with the holidays. Luigi's face, in hospital, had seemed worn out by the heat of August.

"Luigi, what is it?"

"Nothing. Everything is changed. Tell me that
you understand".

The real problem was that she did understand,
she understood very well, even if she would have
done anything not to have to understand.

"She is in the incubator. But she is doing very
well. Everything worked out. I mean she is a seven
month baby, but they say she has the strength of a
normal child. In a short while she will be normal
size, we will take her home and look after her".

"Listen to me, it's not possible. We have given
destiny a hostage. I cannot put myself in the hands
of fate, of the gods who might have taken her away,
not have allowed her to be born, and can strike when
they want. The fact that she was born like this, two
months before her time, is already a sign".

Not for him the precious roundness of Prisca's
gift which she, the girl, had to keep alive in every
way.

Before leaving, he had said:

"Tell me you are not like the other women. That
you will not be only mother and nurse. Tell me that
there are other children: your activity, your work".

The girl would have liked to say: "Let's start with Prisca, Luigi. She is here, she is ours, she is mine". Even if she was a seven month baby, she was her perfect creation, the creation to which she had hoped to give shape.

I must speak with Grandmother, the girl thought, after breastfeeding Prisca and putting her to sleep. It's the first moment of peace I have, the first time I feel that Prisca will make it and will grow as big as the other children, as the other girls who never endured what she had to endure. Grandmother is a bit tired, she seemed only faintly pleased by Prisca's birth. But maybe she was only worried. Of course she will help me without my saying anything, without my saying much.

But there was no time to speak to her or to make a decision about that famous holiday. Before the supermarket closed down and when the pharmacy had already its holiday period, Grandmother took sick. She resisted a while longer, during those summer nights without human sounds, when, next to Anna, the nurse, the girl searched, in the shape abandoned on the bed, for the beautiful woman, for the body she had loved so much. On one of those nights Grandmother recovered and told the girl:

"All will be well".

Then there were only the fingers of a hand, which opened and closed regularly for hours, to show that Grandmother still existed. And, at one point, they too stopped.

Lying down, in her rest, Grandmother became very young again, with an unlined skin, a fresh face, as she had been at the time of her great departures with Enzo. And she left just as the girl had feared she would leave ever since her childhood: forever.

CHAPTER 10

The days of Prisca's first winter at the Colosseo, punctually brought back the memory of the days during the previous winter. Mourning must be this, the persistence of memory, the girl said to herself; one has no peace until one sees the same moons, the same lights come back, and past and present have fully confronted each other without escape and without subterfuge.

The lights, however, were not at all the same. It was a mild and rainy winter; in the streets the sun rose and set at completely different angles, both familiar and unfamiliar, like a life within another life. It was in fact a life that, in spite of Prisca's presence, resembled a hibernation. All came back in a form that was both punctual and deceptive: that week she had gone to Luigi, no, in fact she had gone the previous week. At the time when now she went to fetch Prisca at the Daycare, the previous year, she sometimes used to phone Grandmother in her empty apartment where it seemed that the rings would always last too long and that the answer never came.

The previous year there had been the wait, Prisca was not there. Now the regret, though always carefully warded off, reopened the wound of the loss of Grandmother. The girl did not weigh her achievements, she did not add up her accounts, owing to an ancient prudence rooted in her since childhood, which consisted in taking care only of small expenses, those for the daily shopping.

Day after day, she told herself that Prisca was doing well and by now moved arms and legs with confidence, as the pediatrician too had observed. She had only a slight cold, at the moment. The previous week the weather had been milder and as a result of this the child had gone out more. During these weather changes, Prisca kept growing. The desire that Prisca, born healthy, but premature, born by surprise, should reach normality within the shortest time and should become completely like the other children, conceived and brought to term by more careful mothers, became now the central factor of the girl's life. By now she spoke to herself of Prisca's growing as her getting stronger, with a familiar and euphemistic expression, but in fact she looked at it as a summit to climb, a mountain to conquer. And this task would have been oppressive, if the girl, in her usual way, had not divided it into stages: food, fresh air, walks, sleep.

Just as the previous year, in her solitude, she had devoted herself to the arithmetic of her periods, the diagrams of pills, the cabala of fertile and infertile days, in order to discover whether she was finally pregnant, in the same way the girl now committed herself to the calculation of the weight gained by Prisca, of the breastfeeding to be increased or diminished, of real meals, of the jars of baby food, biscuits, orange juice and ground meat which would have supplemented the breastfeeding and made the child gain weight. She did not speak to anyone of the hours she spent putting her daughter on the scales, comparing her mentally in terms of weight to other children of the same age, wracking her brain about how long it would take for Prisca to fill the gap and make up for the disadvantage she had at the moment of birth.

Even if she was very tired, she did not wish for anyone to distract her from this task of making her daughter grow. She was convinced that this task belonged only to her and that nobody else would be able to understand how long an undertaking it was, one destined never to end. In fact the four-five month old Prisca who weighed seven-eight kilos and had three meals and one breastfeeding a day, would be replaced through the years by many other Priscas, always with programs to be updated and perfected so as to create a daughter who not only did not lack anything, but was the best daughter possible.

This was a program that obsessed her and made her happy at the same time just because it was that program of love and continuous tests that she had anticipated at the very moment of Prisca's birth. Her mother was the only person with whom she succeeded in sharing her concerns about Prisca, even if only moderately. The girl suspected that her Mother, as a young woman and even later, had experienced ambitions and obsessions very similar to hers. But, just because these ambitions had made her suffer in the past and even now kept nagging at her, she tried very hard not to make comparisons. For instance, when her mother with her usual nervousness, ordered her not to take Prisca out because it was raining or the wind was blowing, or when she confided to her, in melodramatic tones that she tried to make lighter, that she found the child pale or lacking an appetite, the girl never failed to rebel. And yet, later on, without even admitting it explicitly to herself, she ended up by agreeing with her mother's opinions and following her advice.

She realized then that a subterranean vein of maternity went back from her to Mother and Grandmother. It was a line that was now taking and had taken a different shape in each of them, but which underlined the fact that they were related, more related and alike than she felt with the women of her own age. And this line was inevitably accompanied by the sense of nature's order, of how life was made and of how days were made for the better and for the worse.

It was very clear to her what Nature was like: nature was Prisca's seductive fragility, the perfume of broom flowers, the passage of clouds that made her think of eternity, the varying of smells, the sensitivity of touch. Her very ordered life was a cage by now. A very narrow cage, with bars that were uneven but all unmoveable: supply teaching, translations, meals, shopping, and Luigi's sudden and unforeseeable calls.

"Well? What does she say?"

"What do you expect her to say? She is four months old".

"But one can hear sounds. You said so yourself".

"Yes, sounds, not words. But she has her own, very beautiful voice, such as I would never have imagined."

"I see" said Luigi. "And when do you predict she'll be able to talk?"

She felt like retorting that she did not predict anything at all, and that it was strange that he should ask this, since he was the last to foresee or even to let people know what would happen the following day. These things that she did not say and did not even utter to herself, contributed to forming the difficult and diffident atmosphere of their telephone calls.

"What about you? Is your work interesting?"

"So, so. Today wasn't bad. Yesterday was very heavy. There was terrible traffic, I was late and the Daycare staff were furious with me; my mother had phoned at least a hundred times to find out what had happened".

"I'm sorry".

The sentence was directed to her or to Prisca, or to both and did not intend to change anything, but it expressed regret and she had accepted it as such. She considered it fortunate not to have to explain to anyone how the game worked between her and Luigi and who, according to her, was suffering a loss and who was not. In fact those around her - and it was a matter of very few people - had given up asking her for an explanation on the subject, and were convinced, the girl thought with bitter pride, that she lived on a totally different planet.

At times, in the evening, when she locked the door after her last return or after mother's or Anna's last visit, and she remained definitely alone, she felt a palpable and pulsating silence. In the small entrance the only voice was and could only be hers, and thus it would remain until morning, while Prisca slept safe and warm in the nearby room. Therefore, finally free, she thought that silence might become part of her creation, with Prisca as well. She was on the stage, as the temporarily free character of a play that, no longer angry, no longer passive, no longer weighed down by memories, could find that happy condition that she had dreamt of so many years before.

But these hours contrasted with other hostile hours which belonged to empty days. They were almost always afternoon hours, when the day was half gone and moved towards an evening without promises. There was, somewhere, a delay impossible to locate, but fatal: a delay in finishing a task, in something that ought to have been done, in occasions that had not been seized, in a life that had taken a new shape. There were noises coming up from the street, but they were frightening noises, of an unfamiliar neighbourhood that the girl had difficulty in recognizing. Silence was not a sign of peace, but of death.

Sometimes she had the sensation that the building was creaking under a storm, or, on the contrary, that she would fall into a chasm without voices and sighs. In reality, during those long days of holidays, the building seemed abandoned by the neighbours, who had run away on their thousand errands, which she daily heard intersecting on the landing: I am going to my aunt, mother wants me tomorrow, my brother in law's sister is in hospital, my husband's niece is receiving Communion. There were special occasions for everyone, deadlines for festivities and bereavements, with obligatory turns and celebrations.

On this agitated Ocean, she and Prisca were almost like two survivors of a shipwreck, at the mercy of a small raft with scant protection: few commitments, few friendships, just a short walk and a visit to her mother, before coming back to the dark harbour of the apartment where she moved in silence, switching on lights, preparing baby bottles, getting things ready.

The obstinate need was that of piercing the silence, of calling out beyond the marsh, where only strangers and people unknown to her seemed to be floating. The more acutely she felt the delay, the emptiness of a useless day that was nearing evening, the more she would have liked to call out again and make herself known. But everyone was really busy, as her mother often observed bitterly, and none cared about what she was doing at that moment.

While those unpleasant, oily hours kept dripping, the girl knew that a happy conclusion would arrive, as it had always done, though every time in a different shape. Once it was an unexpected sound from Prisca, another time it was a cheerful thought, another time again it was her own face in the mirror which suddenly looked attractive. A cruel wind blew over wreckages and regrets. Then there came a call, an invitation to live.

CHAPTER 11

O ne day, towards the end of that winter, she had the impression she saw the girl in black again. But she was not completely certain, because the light, the background or the context in which the event took place was totally different from the encounter at Villa Borghese over a year before, and perhaps the woman she saw was different too.

From her car window, while she was following closely behind a bus that was having difficulty climbing a crowded Via IV Novembre, even at a snail's pace, she found herself looking at the people who were waiting for the bus a little further on. Standing slightly apart from the group there was a figure turned three quarters away. She was not in black, she was all in beige, but once more she wore a kind of uniform from head to foot: a tight-waisted raincoat, trousers, a heavy sweater and a wide brimmed man's hat. It was definitely the girl's hat, though worn in a different way, and hers was also the outline of her forehead to her chin that she had admired from much closer on that November morning. And even if she had not seen the girl's raincoat before, even if it was unfamiliar, she felt that it was typical of the girl to wear her collar raised in a bold masculine fashion. More like an apache than Don Quixote, thought the girl in a quick and fleeting way, while looking at her briefly but with a gaze rendered intense by the desire that the woman should turn and reveal herself in a definitive way. By now the bus, which was in front of her car, had stopped at the stop and since it was crowded, it took a long time for the people to get off. And then a lot of people were trying to get on. But the woman in beige did not get on, although the girl in her car was so eager to see her move and to confirm that in fact it was she. That woman was waiting for another bus, or perhaps, she was not waiting for any bus.

But she did not move and remained fixed, tall and straight, looking at an unknown window or mirroring herself in it, in a pose that did not imprison her but seemed to keep her suspended, ready for a throw, a lift-off flight, an encounter.

At first the girl despaired because the woman's stillness made it impossible to find out whether it was really she. Afterwards, instead, she wanted to persuade herself that the very fact that the woman had not mingled with the crowd in the bus was a sign that she was not lost, sucked up into the void and was instead available, if only for a few seconds: the very short time during which the last people got on the bus, the bus closed its doors and traffic started up again, fatally sucking her and her car into that big snake from which it was impossible to get away. And during the few seconds that she could devote to the persistent contemplation of that motionless figure which, in spite of the distance, had become nearer and clearer as people moved away from it, the girl made a curious discovery. On the nape of her neck, under the gathered hairstyle mostly concealed by hat and collar, there escaped some rebellious curly hair.

She had not seen it in the Italian garden at Villa Borghese; the hat had covered it entirely at the time, whereas this hat was more closefitting and revealed it. That rebellious hair, born from the skin on the nape, and almost skin itself, in its curious vitality sent a message of beauty and love.

The bus closed its doors and started on its way. The girl too was compelled to start the engine and follow the bus, for the other cars behind her were already honking. She had resisted the temptation of honking her horn in order to see the woman better; in that case the figure who was always motionless and three quarters turned would be startled and, whether it was she or not, she would dissolve forever.

In the city traffic, while she was driving in a slow and automatic way, going through traffic-lights, overtaking cars and coming to sudden stops, she continued to see her, even afterwards, standing out against other houses, other intersections, other shop windows. In the back of that bus, as long as she followed it, and then even in other buses there were tired, absent minded, indifferent faces which did not interest her any longer. She was now isolated in the joy of having grasped that strange wonder, and was seized by the desire of giving life to that curious quivering hair which kept asking her to do so. Instead of timetables, duties and fixed routes she saw in front of her rapid images of indefinite patterns, all connected to each other, born and multiplying by themselves, like waves.

The girl suddenly thought: this, after months of mourning, is a desire to love, even if it asks so little from the almost inexistent woman who by now has disappeared into the confusion of an ordinary day. It would be enough for her to find the woman in her pose, the movement of the shadows, the line of the turned cheekbone, and then those rebellious curls above the collar. And to experience the voluptuous pleasure, ancient and bitter companion of all her life, of searching for the perfume of violet on Grandmother's neck or for the soft line of the woman's body, stretched on the mountain.

This desire was also changeable, and could become quite different: it could look on a secluded garden of Eden, which belonged to Lent, with soft, light colours, a premonition of purification. It is February now, thought the girl with a shudder. Anything can happen in this tail end of a season, which is promising as all spare time can be, when nothing finishes and everything starts again and is different, when unfamiliar streets lead into the unknown and look onto unexpected landscapes. The streets on which she travelled pushing Prisca's pram belonged to the realm of dreams and possibilities: grassy slopes, hemmed in by tall walls, or sudden openings of the road in front of churches with very ancient names, or gardens blocked by great walls, beyond which the eye roamed over the city, the bends in the river, the bridges, the banks of the Tiber. She did not and could not find anyone she knew on those slopes, even though she had spent her life in that city. But the city itself appeared overturned to her, now that she saw it from the other side and controlled it from an unexpected height.

Down there, beyond the green mass of Villa Borghese, the landscape included her house, with the streets that belonged to Grandmother, to Enzo, to herself; down there, thanks to the distance, epochs and people were superimposed like geological strata, merging into a coexistence that no longer showed any breaks or chips.

It was like being a little bit dead or extraordinarily powerful, and managing to arrange things the way they were not arranged in everyday life. Down there was the bridge of Pietroburgo, which meant love, embrace, obstinacy, conception, that fury of Luigi that almost did not hurt her any longer and did not correspond to the sweet little face that slept among blankets and hoods in the pram. An then in the Italian garden, with its obsessive continuous design, there were other desires, other more subtle submissions. But the landscape got lost in the distance, to the north, on clear days, towards the Sabine mountains, which she saw from the American school, sprinkled with snow, in winter.

Even more secret patterns might appear, and other desires for love, buried under the leafage of so many seasons, might come back to life.

CHAPTER 12

The cold and the loneliness became less rigid. From the pearly grey there emerged spring shades of green or pink. Grass grew, here and there, in the cracks of the tufa walls, and the trees in the ancient open spaces sprouted buds and leaves. In the days that grew longer and expanded to receive new faces and new sensations, the newest was certainly Prisca. Freed from too many blankets, and emerging from the depths of her cradle and of her pram, now she found a direct contact with the world in her stroller. She sat waving her hands, she took off the hood of her jacket, she made faces when she was tired and when the sun shone in her eyes, she smiled at everyone, especially at the girl, and said: "Look, Mummy, yum-yum" and a few more words. These expressions astounded the public because of their completeness and precocity, but she, the girl, found them completely natural.

"Seven months".

The others were full of admiration and stopped mother and daughter in the street, by their house, in the stores, in front of the nursery, and treated them as local celebrities.

"Seven months, look how lively, beautiful and smart she is, what a darling, how sweet she is, how lovely".

The girl nodded silently, out of politeness, not wanting to appear vain or proud. Since she was happy about the praises that were directed to her daughter, she easily showed the joy and satisfaction

which were required by the occasion, thereby elicit-
ing even greater praises and sympathy. However she
could not confess to anyone that she was immensely
proud of her daughter and that those praises seemed
quite natural to her, in fact barely sufficient. In the
bottom of her heart, in fact, she was absolutely convinced that Prisca knew and understood everything
by now and that only a feeling of propriety, not
unlike her own, prevented the child from showing
herself as aware and intelligent as her mother, of
whom she was certainly the mirror image.

In fact the girl suddenly saw in Prisca her own
childhood and felt that they were both living and
seeing a well known period of her own life again and
starting together on a familiar route. In the girl's
imagination, Prisca was not seven months old, she
was two, three, five. In fact it was not Prisca, it was
the girl herself with her mother in an undefined season, a kind of no man's land between America and
Italy, between decks of ships and plane seats, during
crossings with many stops and landings in unknown
cities, where her mother kept recreating the same
atmosphere, a mixture of solitude and mutual solidarity. She did not remember specific cities and
years, rather she remembered moments of silence
and endurance, things that were concealed, loyalties divided between two continents, as well as
festivities, celebrations and ceremonies.

At the end of May or at the beginning of June, at
the American school, one Saturday afternoon was
given up to a fair, a notion that Cesira did not understand at all and that even Gradmother reduced to
the level of activity for charity. Only she and Mother
understood that it was a rural celebration of spring
and summer and belonged only to the two of them.
The booths were set up in the garden of the school,
an Italian villa with turrets and terraces, in the mid-

dle of fields of poppies and yellow daisies, with heavy white clouds hanging in the sky, against the background of the Sabine region and of Mt. Soratte. She and her Mother were the only ones who knew that this fair encompassed all the fairs they had seen together in the past and that were blooming in those same days in every corner of America. This fair had the same long tables laid with home baked cakes, with red and white candies and marshmallows, the same games, the same competitions and the same public. The men wore short-sleeved shirts that were too large for them, and the women, on the contrary, were too dressed up, with their gloves, stiletto heels and falsetto voices. As in other fairs, people were good-natured and easily pleased by bingo games and races; they enjoyed food and beverages which were similar to their home-cooking. But for the girl and her mother this food remained new and pioneer-like, connected with the memories of a friendly fairy story, where there were picnic tables, lit up fires in a welcoming wood on the outskirts of a town made of little houses all looking the same.

That long summer afternoon represented a happy combination of destiny, in which every regret and every loss ceased to exist and was replaced by the feeling of having reached a high point. These two different lives and national loyalties joined together and enhanced each other. And even if the archetype, the leafy American wood, was very beautiful, this Roman version of it was infinitely more attractive, given the mood that pervaded it throughout, in a silent and obscure way.

"It's a privilege" said the Americans, pensively savouring potato salad, hot dogs, lemon pie and Seven Up.

"A real privilege. At least that's what I think. Rome. The eternal city. The Pope."

"A privilege. Everything is so beautiful. It has been a good year. We have been so happy. A very good year, in fact an extraordinary one. How beautiful to live between the mountains and the Mediterranean."

Even domestic geography assumed grand characteristics, with borders and civilizations that for once were not at war with each other, but were happily united under the sign of the American way to peace and happiness. The sky turned dark blue, the golden light of the Roman countryside bathed the almost empty the tables, the colourful tablecloths, the glasses and paper plates, the read and white candies and the Japanese lanterns that had not yet been lit. The air carried a very strong perfume of honeysuckle, laurel, linden and broom, but also contained the memory of different scents, the damp heat wave of the young American summer in the faraway Continent. A unique and unrepeatable moment, that took place between one season and another, in a fleeting moment.

"Our stay has been a privilege, an unforgettable and priceless experience" the Americans repeated, looking straight at Mother, in an intense way, with the certainty of being completely understood.

"We wouldn't have missed it for anything in the world, we will remember it all our lives".

Her mother understood the Americans and spoke the same happy and slightly bombastic language. She was well aware of the exceptional conjunction of the stars. Her mother stood out in the crowd for her perfect looks. She was still young, had no thick and ridiculous perms and wore very beautiful Italian shoes and bags.

"Where did you buy them?" murmured the other mothers: "They are beautiful, really beautiful".

She gave them names, addresses and explanations. Her mother directed the other ladies towards newly opened boutiques and offered them her help and company in case they wanted to go there with her. They all took careful notes in their tidy notebooks, crammed with bits of information, even if they were certain that it would be completely useless.

In fact nothing would ever happen and they would never meet again as on that magic May evening. In all probability they would never see each other again. In fifteen, twenty days the American ladies would leave with their husbands and their many blonde and toothy children. They would return to their modest little houses, built in a row, from where they would never again admire Mt. Soratte or the Alban Mountains. Entire families moved to the four corners of the world where there were other schools, other American colonies, other fairs.

The school changed every year with new and different children. Only they, the fake Americans, the half-castes, like the girl and Davy, met each other with some humiliation, every September, year after year. But for the moment this was faraway. Long and lasting relationships seemed possible and far off the departures and the returns across the Ocean. The difficult necessities of choices, separations, nationalities and passports were temporarily cancelled.

"We must meet again".

"We must. It was so beautiful".

"It was so exciting. We must form a group, an association of American children and parents. We can ask for subsidies and organize lectures and lunches".

For one moment the mother and the daughter believed it too. In reality the gatherings with the Italian children, sons of family friends, were complicated and boring. And the atmosphere of that horrible Parioli Square was oppressive. Here instead, during the fair, in the mock Renaissance villa with the stars and stripes waving proudly above it, everything spoke of the eternal freedom of travelling and learning.

Little by little the party came to an end and the fairy tale Japanese lanterns were lit. The voices died down and the calls of the children playing the games became rarer. At intervals the large Buicks, Mercuries, and Fords screeched over the gravel at the entrance and after a moment's hesitation turned onto Via Cassia, in the direction of Rome. At that point the girl too would have liked to finish the day, so that she might immediately start to remember it.

"Let's go away" said Mother. "It's really late".

The feverish excitement of the party had abated, the last goodbyes became more painful, with shy kisses exchanged on a single cheek and declarations of friendship sounded like farewells. In the darkening evening, they would walk away to the parking lot, clinging to each other, and get into their small car.

"It was wonderful" Mother would say, turning on the engine. "A really wonderful party".

There was no need for her to answer: she was in perfect agreement.

The world of the fair lasted as far as the city gates, until they could see the yellow fields of stubbles and the outline of the mountains and smell distant perfumes in the air. It was an immense and solitary countryside which was waiting to welcome the lovers during its long night.

"It has been wonderful," Mother repeated.

But she said it for the last time. Houses began to appear now and new apartment buildings and the usual street that ended up in Parioli Square, amid plane trees, stadiums and racetracks. They would not have been able to explain even to Grandmother what they had experienced that afternoon. It would not have been worth their while.

But in their joint life of mother and daughter something had gone wrong fairly early. The hopes of childhood, of the heroic period of journeys, of shared loneliness, of mother's precepts and stories had all been lost. The girl thought that even for Mother there existed a fair, even though it was a different one from hers and even though nowadays she would refer to it with annoying sentences. That fair was a unique moment in which her condition of young woman living alone had become a mirror for her child and the horizon had narrowed around them.

She did not know who had been the first to disappoint the other: maybe everything had been due to Mother's marriage to Giovanni, or to the fact that she had become close to Grandmother, or to Enzo's love for Grandmother, or to her own love, when she was a child, for Enzo and Grandmother, or to all these things put together. It was a tangled mass that separated and united them at the same time and that prevented them from enjoying their feelings, unless they received some approval from the others. Perhaps even Grandmother, who seemed so free, had suffered from the same illness. And maybe in some crucial occasion, Mother and Grandmother had judged the girl by the same yardstick.

As she pondered these and other matters, her heart sank, or at least she saw the same ground, the same point of view. A kind of foreshortening of a

Parioli courtyard with the two apartments almost facing each other and their comings and goings, departures, arrivals and return, over a period of many years, with a uniform and repetitive rhythm.

And yet analogies and repetitions had not finished and when Prisca had suddenly blossomed; Mother had also formed a particular relationship with the baby and considered her exploits quite natural and not at all surprising. With the passing years her mother had acquired the need to show off everything that she, instead, liked to keep hidden. As a result, Mother did not hesitate to proclaim to Anna and to the other neighbours in the apartment building, and probably also to Giovanni and other people, when she was alone with them, the incontrovertible fact that Prisca was a genius and that it would have been really strange if it had been otherwise. But the girl understood well that her mother's words went beyond Prisca and referred to the brilliance and extraordinary qualities of her own daughter, who had wasted and kept on wasting those qualities day after day, even to the very moment at which Mother was talking.

It was impossible to unravel old and new features, just as happens when people resemble each other. In Prisca's little face she did not know whether to find herself, or Luigi, or a mixture of herself and Luigi, or simply a third person quite distinct from the other two and from all the numberless other people who had created her through the years and the centuries.

When it seemed to her that her mother fussed over Prisca, spoke to her and cuddled her just as she had done with her in the past, at the moment when she might have become a child again with Prisca, something changed. The tone, the voice, were dictated by the day, the time, the place. At that moment neither America nor Italy existed any longer, nor the people with whom they had talked in the past, nor Mother's girl friends, nor the nannies in Villa Borghese. However much she identified with Prisca, her working-class apartment building near the Colosseo would never be able to give her back her past, now that voices and lights had changed from that time, as had the baby food, the teething biscuits and the toys.

She and her mother moved over new territory, in a slightly false atmosphere that softened the blows. Prisca's growth and beauty, which made them both proud, was certainly an essential element of that atmosphere. But it was equally important that they no longer lived together, but paid each other rather ceremonious and sad visits, in which those who were absent surfaced in their thoughts: Grandmother, first of all, and then Luigi and even Giovanni, who turned up very rarely.

The girl for the moment had no fair to offer Prisca, who, from her stroller, looked at her and called to her with trust and persistence and who stretched her hands towards the walls, the grass and the children. The fair was not there nor was Deer Park, where, among spaces between the holm oaks, she had invented a space which replaced Grandmother's appearances and disappearances towards a love nest. Now the ships and the planes of her childhood were missing too, along with her feelings of devotion to Mother and the need to protect Mother from knowing how visible were her efforts to protect her child. She had nothing to offer her, except for the prospect of the very long season of childhood through which they would go together: a period which had to be settled, concealed, mediated with great effort and without great success, just as her Mother had done.

She had nothing for Prisca: unless that fair or other fairs, which were unknown to her at the moment, would come into being by themselves. Perhaps those fairs would materialize out of spring days, like that Sunday at the end of February, out of the faraway magic noises of the city beyond the river, and out of the very fact that she and Prisca, mother and daughter, looked into each other's faces and smiled, while one pushed the stroller and the other let herself be pushed.

CHAPTER 13

The girls did everything: some pruned, wearing big gloves and holding garden shears, with their thin legs spread a little apart, in their calf length pants. One of them, with long hair, raised her arm to hold her piqué cap. She was warding away the gust of wind that, when she got on the boat, would swell her striped shirt on her small breasts and on her thin torso, which appeared as a triangle between the shirt knot and the pants low on the hip. But not many of them were ready for the open air life, because winter had come back and an icy wind blew, lifting whirls of dust mixed with big drops.

Almost all the other girls wore play outfits as well, but more suited to the season: tender and soft suede buck, in pale colours never seen before; a very delicate grey; a brown that combined the colours of the camel, the hazelnut and the sand; a shiny black; an all new and flaming red; and a special pink which was different from the pink of the previous year and in fact from any other pink. These were colours and shades to be savoured with gluttony, like ice creams to be licked, that would give rise to unforeseen sensations, always tasting of nostalgia and memory.

The girls were ready for trips and adventure, with their travelling bags, which were soft, but easy to carry and ready to contain intimate belongings, make up and pills. The girls were adaptable: now they were lion tamers, with their tight trousers stuck inside high boots, now they were the wonderful companions of a thousand excursions. They were always consenting, always gregarious, always available to changing plans, with a mystery that remained, however, between their half closed eyes and their partly opened lips. The mystery was not present in their bodies where the contrast between high and low parts, shoulders and breasts, hips and legs was emphasized, but also made banal by cuts, breaks and the play of colour: red black, blue beige, yellow white. Rather it was present in the way in which the girls took part in what they were doing or were about to do, in the way in which they bent their serious and gloomy faces forward.

Or perhaps the mystery was simply in the grand game that at that moment everybody everywhere in the city was playing: in all the downtown shop windows, in the Corso and in the streets that ran into it and then extended all over to the shining stores in the many suburbs and areas near Rome. They all played that game and seemed to know its rules, which, however, they made up perhaps as they went along, in order to be part of the game.

All those girls resembled her students, even if they were taller and slimmer. They wore blouses decorated with designs, squares, stripes: shapes and colours variously put together and combined in an endless and forever changing topography. They wore ruffled underclothes, Turkish style pants and little low-waisted dresses with red, yellow and green frills on slender bodices. Such preparation and such fantasy seemed destined to a rather modest activity: daytrips, excursions outside the city gates, or the pleasure of wandering around in an aimless way. They seemed to be just like school girls who, after many hours spent in the same classroom, suddenly switched off their attention and, without a word of greeting or recognition, got onto a roaring scooter behind a boy. They had the same reserved and tense expression, which however belied the way in which they kept obstinately close to their boyfriends, and tightened their muscles on the scooter as if it were a love embrace.

"May I help you?"

The voice came from very near and, though it was quite low, it succeeded in piercing the rock music, by adapting to it rather than struggling with it. And in fact every element there was reflected into the next one and adapted to it: it was reflected in the mirrors and was matched by the heavy and soft wall-to-wall carpeting. The long intersecting rows of dresses, sports shirts, pants, patterns, stripes, squares, waves, bags, scarves, were continued by the images of the women who were looking from the outside, with their long hair, narrow faces, new pants and jackets. And they in turn got mixed up with the other women who wandered among the rows of garments and wore the same clothes as the women outside.

The wall-to-wall carpeting muffled the footsteps and let the music dominate. In some way, in spite of the noise, people were silent and listening, as if they were going into a confessional. The women were going back and forth among the clothes and the mirrors. They looked at the garments, felt them and sometimes they took two or three in their arms, and with a brief nod to someone, they disappeared: as if they were going into a confession booth. At the cash register there was a young girl, who wore an enormous clumsy jacket patterned with lozenges in strident colours, revealing her light and shiny shirt. She was not the girl in black. If she had ever been there, she had left no trace of her presence.

"May I help you?"

No woman in there resembled her fantasies: no woman would have been able to press her pubis on the ground and penetrate it, or wrap herself in uniforms of mystery and domination. They were small fry: they liked working-class amusements, spangles, tigers, fake Oriental patterns, head covers which tried to imitate Isadora Duncan's fatal veils, materials which were horrible to touch, rough stitching, synthetic products. It was the nightmare through which she lived daily in the streets, at school, in her apartment building near the Colosseo. A nightmare which drove her back into her own desires and isolation and rendered communication so difficult. She did not even understand why she had entered a similar nightmare and yet she felt her feet glued to the carpet on the floor and was unable to go out.

"May I help you?"

Behind her stood the person who had spoken. Another girl, of course. She saw her at first in one of the mirrors which doubled the real world, by creating an exact copy of it: same dresses, colours and combinations of patterns. At first she had difficulty in distinguishing her, since the picture in the mirror was as crowded as the scene at a rock concert or at a beach but with fully-dressed people. The person who stood out clearly had a washed out colour, a face different from the others and lacked their ability to dress up for a part. But in this case as well she had difficulty in recognizing herself: it was her face, it was she, the teacher of her students, the mother of Prisca. She did not even resemble her mother at present, and even less her mother as a young woman. In a short while she would no longer have a place in that world where they all wore the uniforms of love, of travelling, of cheerfulness. The wolf jacket went back to an epoch of which they had lost any memory in that rag fair. In any case she knew perfectly well that there was nothing less fashionable than a relatively recent fashion, nothing more off, more out of date and less likely to be revived. Her clothes had that grey, uncertain look that belonged to the periods before, during and after her pregnancy. They denounced traumas and desertions. They were just something to wear while she made an effort to communicate at any cost.

"I don't know".

She meant to say: "Nothing suits me here. I had better look among the best materials and sober styles and choose one thing that may cost a fortune and last for years." Then all of a sudden she did not even want that classic uncompromising style in black or beige. The girl was staring at her and the deafening music continued to produce ritual gestures. People came in and asked questions. Figures moved slowly from one counter to the other, with a soft, automatic, fatal motion, pre-arranged in the horrifying circuit of consumer society.

"There are the new suits: two or three pieces, with their jackets. They are fun and have just arrived. We have also coordinates, with trousers and long jackets. You can wear the jacket separately.

She moved towards a row of garments which she would never have been able to spot by herself. She looked at her briefly from top to bottom, to gage her size. She let herself be looked at by those clear, black eyes, beneath the grand hairstyle of black, curly locks, which were turned, waved and sculpted so as to make her look like Medusa. Otherwise she resembled everybody else in the store, with her slim hips invitingly rounded by ballooning khaki pants which tightened up on her thin ankles and boots. She wore a large decollete top, decorated with gold and silver.

"May I look around?"

"Certainly. Let me know if you need anything. I am here".

The others did everything by themselves: they were very young, almost children. She thought of the little girls who played with the same skilful and maniacal concentration in the courtyard of her building. They were small but already had nimble fingers, with which they dressed and undressed their tall dolls with such long and perfect bodies, small breasts, small buttocks, flat pelvises, so sexy that their sex no longer existed.

But once more, in her unease, she was almost an anomaly, a kind of replica of her mother, and she was not so prehistoric as to be fashionable again. In the courtyard the lingering and nimble movements of the girls' fingers, their heads with long, straight hair, which sometimes looked like the exact copy of their dolls' head, set her into a state of erotic anxiety, without granting her any relief. Here, instead, she felt a certain pleasure in observing these grown-up girls bustling around with clothes their own size. These protagonists were very serious and skilful in choosing a dress. They pressed it against their bodies in front of a mirror, half closed their eyes and imagined they were wearing it on a particular occasion: on a motor bike, on the beach, at a meeting, in a pizza parlour, at a wedding or at the first communion of their brother-in-law's sister. They fixed their scarves and belts, while gracefully moving their shoulders, breasts or hips. Their graceful bodies moved by themselves, as in a dance, without any need to be enhanced, but received the unexpected gift of seduction from a garment with pattern, colour and design planned in some unknown location, and made by some illegal, underground establishment in some part of Italy or of the world. For them this was a storehouse of organized and preordained pleasures, which they alone would be able to use, adapt, put on and take off. They had the ritualistic confidence which is typical of women who practice an intricate and closed activity: housewives, nuns and prostitutes.

"So, how do you like them?"

She had in fact chosen some clothes: the most faded and least beautiful colours in that shining parade, the most subdued fashion among those little masterpieces in style and combination. She was trying to hide, to disappear, not to reveal in any way to the girls that she was competing with them, in the same way as she concealed herself from the very young people she taught in school.

But even these clothes were too much for her. She was discouraged by everything: the heat of the changing room, the obsessive light of the mirrors, the music which was even louder here, and her own body which appeared strange to her after her childbirth. In the apartment near the Colosseo, in the empty and silent rooms, while Prisca was asleep, the dim lights rendered her appearance more bearable and made her hope that she would reacquire the looks she had before Prisca was born. Now, however, the cruel comparison with all those very young girls revealed to her that her body was nothing. It was not even old. It was insipid and non existent, like her life and like the long joyless years still to come, in the midst of a very precocious middle age.

"I don't like them at all".

She did not want to be seen even by her. She tried to grab her old and familiar skirt and sweater and get dressed again, covering herself in a hurry.

Instead the young girl had come with other clothes: bright, springlike, almost summery. She closed the door behind her, with a firm movement of her back, and hung the clothes.

"Why? Come on, try this".

They stared at each other for a moment in the mirror that had placed them one next to the other and where they did not even look incongruous. The salesgirl handed her the various clothes. She did not offer any explanation for the white pants or for the pink pants. The choice was obviously meant neither for the present cold weather nor for the immediate future.

"They are a bit light".

"Easter is approaching. Surely you'll be going out".

It was an illusion, but it flattered her. As soon as it was in contact with those different things, her body adjusted to them and became lighter.

"I don't know" she tried again.

"They are darling" the other said with authority. "Take the shirt too. Wait. I am going to choose a jacket for the colder evenings for you".

She offered a final resistance

"They are transparent".

The girl shrugged her shoulders.

"All you need is to wear some matching under-wear".

With a sharp movement she pulled down the zipper of her jeans and revealed a very white little belly, a dark pubis and black pubic hair escaping out of her yellow g-string.

"Simona, you are wanted on the phone" someone called from outside.

"Can you take the call for me? I am busy now".

They remained in silence, keeping a common secret.

"I'll take everything" the girl said.

Slowly Simona started gathering the things, while the girl took off her pants with equal slowness.

"Do you need anything else?"

"No".

There was no point in lying to her and telling her: "For the time being". She would never come back there.

She looked at her for the last time while she was paying at the cash desk.

Outside the wind had dropped and the sky was lying heavy above her, grey but full of peace. The girl was walking fast, feeling light, not lonely and slightly excited.

She looked for a pay phone in a coffee bar.

Mother said:

"All is well here. Prisca has eaten and now she is asleep. Luigi phoned. He will call back later in the evening".

Then she added:

"It started to snow here. Prisca saw the snow and enjoyed it very much. Take it easy, don't hurry back, darling. Leave everything to me".

For a moment it seemed to her she heard Grandmother speaking, but then she did not think of it any more. There too it had started snowing: a few large snowflakes. The appearance of the streets was changing from one minute to the next, and people were changing too. Little by little it became a different city.

She lifted her head to feel the snow that was streaming from her hair to her chin, but, while she was walking, she was tempted to glance at what she had bought. The light materials immediately got wet, but they were just as attractive as she remembered them. Prisca, on the other hand, needed a dress: she was a child, she was big by now. And the girl was already imagining Prisca's round knees peeking out below the hem.

1.   The sit-in mentioned here refers to the revolt of the students which took place in Italy between 1967 and 1968. Highschool and university students occupied their classrooms and demonstrated against their professors in order to protest the overcrowding of their schools, the poor training of their teachers, the unfair system of exams used in university and the lack of good jobs for those who finally got their degrees. This revolt had also an ideological basis since "the values of solidarity, collective action and the fight against social injustice were counterposed to the individualism and consumerism of 'neo-capitalism'." Paul Ginsborg, *A History of Contemporary Italy*, London: Penguin Books, 1990, p. 301.